The Art of Cheating Episodes: S1E4

KeLLy's Revenge

EXTENDED AUTHOR'S CUT EDITION

HoLLyRod

COPYRIGHT

April 2012

You never think it could happen to you.

That's the only way a nigga can live like this. Night after night, you gotta find a way to trick yourself into believing that you somehow exempt from the consequences. It's best to have a short memory. When you can easily forget about the shit you out here doing, it's almost impossible to develop that guilty conscience that keeps you from going too far again. The best cheaters learn how to master this technique of being forgetful early. It's the key to keeping your sanity when you're playing around with so many hearts in the *Art*.

I never had the luxury. My memory bank runs too deep and I remember most things like they happened yesterday. Pops used to tell me to look at that as my strength. He always said the *Son's Curse* forced you to reflect for the better. But at the same time, neither Pops nor Grandpa Jerry had found a way to counter the energy behind the *Curse* – not like I had done with the *Art of Cheating*. Some shit *needed* to be forgotten about, at least momentarily. My inner ~~beast~~ always helped with that part of the game.

"Why the fuck she keep calling me like this, bro?!?" I curl my lip at the phone vibrating again in the passenger seat.

"Just answer it, nigga," the voice whispers with identical irritation. *"What you scared of? I'm tired of her ass calling, too."*

This *is* like the fifth time she's called. It's not that I'm scared to answer though. My brain is just racing, caught up in these thoughts. Answering any calls right now would simply break the inkling of concentration I've managed to hold on to all night.

"Ain't nobody scared, dawg. Shut that shit up."

This rain is really pouring down now. I truly hate how much it storms this time of year. Missouri weather is the worst. It can be sunny and clear one minute and then, out of nowhere, it's either snowing or raining. Temperature can go up or down 20 degrees somedays. I fuckin' hate it here.

It's just after **3:30am** and now I'm starting to sober up too much. I prolly shoulda popped some more pills before I got on the road, honestly. The thumping in my heart gets worse with each passing moment and I can only pray that it doesn't turn into a panic attack on this foggy highway. Lord knows that's the last thing I need right now.

It's been months since I've had an attack. Last year it was damn near once a week. Between mourning deaths, dodging jail from Ronnie's situation, and dealing with Sug's crazy ass…I had more than the average share of stressful nights. When Dr. Julie first diagnosed me with my anxiety and PTSD issues back in '07, I was in complete denial and refused to take the meds. Last year – all'at shit changed. Now I can't stop chewing these muhfuckaz like candy.

I been doing a lot better lately though, especially these last couple of months without Sug around. Finding the will to let her walk away seemed like such the right move at the time. My creative juices were back flowing. My energy was up. I was starting to see clearly again, the belligerent clouds beginning to fade. My broken cheater's heart had finally begun to heal.

"Yeah, but you just had to answer the phone again when she called…didn't you Rod?" the **beast** reminds me mercilessly.

When Sug called me out the blue last week, I'll admit I couldn't bring myself to ignoring the call. I missed her…I missed the strange connection we had. Even knowing how much bullshit we had put each other through and how detachment made sense for the two of us, when I saw her name flash across my screen…I answered without hesitation.

"Come on, bro! I ain't know it was gon go down like this, dawg," I try to convince myself.

"Nigga, I told you not to trust her ass, HoLLy. I told you in the beginning when you fell for the bitch, like I told yo ass last week when she popped up outta nowhere. Don't trust that hoe. I told you, nigga."

He ain't telling no lies. From the first moment I started to feel some type of emotional connection towards Sug, I could hear that voice in the back of my head going off. Something about Suga B never sat right with my **beast**…which is saying a lot. At the same time however, there was something about Sug that drew my inner **beast** in, right along with my more vulnerable side.

"Aww, don't act like I was the only one down with it! You saw opportunity just like I did, nigga. Out for blood, remember?"

"Yeah, but still... what did I say? I said keep it MOBAN and stick to the plan. What I say? No emotions this time, HoLLy! Focus on the money!"

"Easier said than done though, bro," I counter to myself. *"It was a risk from the jump. We both knew that. You just never think it could happen to you. Not like this."*

The brief silence is broken with my phone ringing, yet again. I know who it is, there's no reason to look. Carmen's been calling off and on since I left her spot earlier tonight...but in the last 20 minutes, it's been back-to-back. I know she's just worried about what I'm gonna do because of how pissed I was when I stormed out.

"I'm not 'bout to answer, bro. Fuck that."

"Nigga, answer the fucking phone before I do," the voice threatens. *"She might have some more intel, fool."*

Maybe, but I doubt it. Carmen spilled a lot of beans tonight, and I drilled the fuck outta her before grabbing my keys to hit this road. So, what else could she possibly have to tell me? She's just tryna calm me down, I'm already knowing.

"She just wanna check on me, bruh. You heard her before I ran out the door. She said, 'Don't do nothing stupid, boo'. That's cuz she know what's bout to go down, nigga. She know Sug got me fucked up."

I still can't stop beating myself up over the fact that I shoulda seen this shit with Sug coming. It's like…you just never think it could happen to you. I can't seem to think straight when it comes to her ass. Hell, even Carmen couldn't believe me earlier when I told her I was really back in KC with Sug again. To the general public, as of last year, HoLLy and Sug were history. And in *my* mind, we finally *were* history after that last fight. I had truly started to move on.

Like Pops, my therapist Dr. Julie was also big on continuous self-reflection and adamant about acknowledging the possibility of karma behind one's actions. Even if I never broke it down in full to her, she always encouraged me to continue to break things down for myself whenever I felt overwhelmed.

Break it down again, Rod. Over and over. Keep breaking this shit down, bro.

My break-up with Sashé had left me bitter and out for revenge. Committed to the *Silent Promise*, I tried to rebuild a new roster of hoes and went on a crazy, careless streak of boldness. But playing with that energy had been dangerous, and the rollercoaster with Sug made that loud and disrespectfully clear.

I walked into 2012 with what felt like a fresh start. Technically single again; this time with slightly less evil intent. Other than Lisa's sister, Shonne, my roster had been all but cleared. Shit almost felt balanced again though – so having Shonne in my pocket was enough to keep my beast fed. But then the night Shonne cancelled our fuck session over a guilty conscious shifted the tide. When Shonne got on her bullshit, I called Carmen as a backup that night. The thing is though – I hadn't fucked with Carmen in over a year after constantly fighting with Sug about our closeness.

You see, Sug and I had a belligerent chemistry that led us down a path you only see in movies. It all moved so fast. First, the both of us found ourselves in a huge financial bind right before my sister Ronnie came home from prison on probation. Then, through a strange sequence of events, by the spring of 2010, we started getting money from Sug selling pussy. About a month into that hustle, Sug and I decided to bring *more* girls on board to expand the money team. **Carmen** was one of those girls.

Now, since Carmen was technically one of my recruits, Sug only extended her trust so far. It wuttin' that she ain't trust me around the other girls – in fact, Sug *expected* me to fuck other bitches. Sug's thing was, she didn't trust the other girls around *me*.

The game Sug and I were playing was unorthodox. It's hard to make a long story short – but at one point, we had a house full of hoes selling ass. There were house rules that applied to everybody in the *Kweens Kwarters*, but one stuck out the most:

*Fucking anybody **for free** outside of our circle was off-limits.*

Sug had this routine when we were choosing new girls...where she would ask them bluntly if they wanted to fuck HoLLy. It was a trick question to create a circle of trust, one in which she always expected the answer to be *'yes'*. Sug would then tell the girls that she didn't blame them, and they should see for themselves what the dick was like. It was Sug's way of telling the other girls that it would take much more than giving HoLLy some pussy to take her spot as the bottom bitch. She wanted them to know that she had no worries about any of them disrupting what we had built together.

But the night I introduced Carmen to Sug, Carmen answered the question wrong.

To have peace in the *Kweens Kwarters* required a level of openness that was far greater than things were in comparison to my previous open relationship with Sashé. This was bigger than sexcapades and ménages. *No lies* really meant *no lies*. From the moment Carmen told Sug that she *didn't* wanna fuck HoLLy, she was on Sug's shit list.

It started off subtle and I'm not sure Carmen even noticed when she first started working with us. Sug was just extra hard on the girl – criticizing her makeup and complaining about the way Carmen talked to the clients, for instance. She thought Carmen's food expenses were too expensive for what she was bringing in. She wouldn't let me defend her...she always disagreed when I told her Carmen was new to the life and just needed time to adjust.

xi

Sug even went as far as accusing me of being soft on Carmen. She felt like I was showing favoritism to a bitch who wuttin' down for the cause like the rest of us in the house.

By mid-summer 2010, we all started to get along more, and I thought the petty rivalry had ended. Then I made the mistake of getting too comfortable with Carmen, provoking Sug to blatantly snap on her in front of the whole *Kwarters*. This led to a big fight with Sug threatening to kick Carmen off the team unless she proved her worth and loyalty over the next 48 hours. Carmen was given an ultimatum and nearly impossible quota to fill, and I made matters worse when I helped her secure her spot in our circle that weekend. From that point on, things just got progressively worse.

By Fall 2010, my sister Ronnie was back in trouble with the police again. In the blink of an eye, the house of hoeing that Sug and I had built from the ground up imploded. Pressure from the police re-opening investigations on my family had Sug ready to move out of the *Kweens Kwarters* and turn over a new leaf. A leaf that she felt she needed to leave me behind for.

I wasn't ready to let her go. After another big fight, we agreed to leave everything in the past and stay together. However, as always, things with Sug rarely came without terms and conditions. She suddenly wanted to completely leave the money-chasing behind and live a square life. In addition to that, she told me that if we were going to work things out, I had to cut off all contact with Carmen going forward.

Reluctantly, but desperately, I gave her what she wanted. Heading into 2011, Sug and I both moved to Saint Louis and left all our belligerent history with Kansas City behind. Not only did I cut off Carmen, I cut off nearly any female I had prior dealings with back home in KC. My inner beast thought I was crazy. My folks back home thought I had finally lost my mind.

After that, it seemed like everything I was doing started backfiring and I was surrounded by all the dark, misfortunate energy. The changes I'd tried to make for Sug were in vain, as we kept clashing. The back-to-back deaths; the writer's block that followed. I started skipping therapy with Dr. Julie, popping more pills, and drinking more heavily. Then I woke up one day and put all of the blame on the music…instead of accepting the possibility of karma for the way I was living.

You never think it could happen to you.

Retiring from the music didn't make things any better and the fights with Sug continued throughout the year. Slowly but surely though, I somehow started to find the strength to let her go. So when we had our last fight at the end of 2011, I truly felt like that was the end of an era.

Lisa's sister Shonne was supposed to be helping me get back to being my less belligerent self again. I mean, she didn't sign up for the job…but still. By the time this new year started, that's what Big Booty Shonne had become my catalyst for. I knew the whole affair was ornery, with her being the older sibling of an old flame. But fucking sisters was still far less ornery than the road I had traveled down with Sug into the underworld. In an attempt to pick up the pieces, I had chosen the lesser of my evils.

Nothing lasts forever...and I've always known that. But Shonne disrupted our thing before I was ready. And since I didn't have any other regulars at the time...I reacted the only way I knew how. Sug was no longer around, so there was no reason to be hesitant about fucking with Carmen again...right?

You would think. So why am I hesitant about answering the phone right now...with Carmen blowing me up like this?

Part of me now feels like when I called Carmen that night Shonne was tripping, I might've reopened that door with Sug unknowingly. At the time I couldn't see it. It wasn't until last week, when Sug called me after months of no contact between each other.

Seeing Sug's name on the screen last Tuesday stopped me in my tracks. But hearing her voice on the other end of the phone truly made me weak. Before she even told me the reason she was calling, the chances of me turning down whatever she was selling were already slim. When she finally said what was on her mind after the brief small talk, I couldn't say no.

Sug had a proposition for me last week, to set all our differences to the side and finish what we had started before moving to Saint Louis.

An opportunity had presented itself back home in Kansas City, and Sug had this bright idea that we should work together one last time to take advantage of it. In spite of the toxic relationship we'd had, when it came to the hustle of getting money together – HoLLy and Sug were a match made in heaven. She knew that I knew that much…if I didn't agree with anything else about us.

"Just one more, HoLLy," she said to me, in her signature charming tone.

Before I knew it, we were on the highway again, back on our bullshit. But little did I realize what the next two days would bring…or how big of a mistake I was making in trusting Sug's energy again. You never think it could happen to you – the betrayal, the type of ulterior motives that only *you're* used to having.

Now I'm flying down the road, back to Saint Louis, chasing Sug down in one last desperate attempt to save face once and for all.

Tonight is filled with irony.

If it wasn't for Carmen, I might've still been in Kansas City right now, clueless to what Sug was plotting. If I hadn't been still in contact with Carmen, giving her the **wooD** from time to time, Sug's plan would've worked without interference. Through crazy coincidence, when I mysteriously couldn't get in touch with Sug earlier tonight, Carmen called my cell phone to 'check up on me'. If Sug hadn't just hung up on me literally seconds prior, I might not have even answered. And if I didn't reveal to her that I was back in town for the weekend, Carmen would've never told me to come see her. She woulda never been able to show me what she had in her possession.

I saw snapshots of Sug's diary tonight with my own eyes. I read firsthand what she had been plotting for months; I saw her intricate plan to destroy me. Before I knew it, I was back in *MyPrecious* and speeding back to Saint Louis, with enough rage to kill this bitch Sug.

"So why won't you answer Carmen's call again then, HoLLy?" the beast wonders. *"I must've missed that part."*

*"Because now I've seen that **Warrensburg** sign again, nigga. Now I'm worried that tonight has even deeper meaning than I thought at first. Now I'm thinking about **KeLLy's Revenge** and what that night led to. Ignoring the signs of the **Curse** never got us anywhere. Carmen can wait a few, I need to hear myself think."*

I've been here before. The energy from my mistakes has obviously re-emerged as a deja vü when I least expected it. And if I can't sort this shit out before I catch up with Sug in the Lou tonight, my next mistake could very well be my last. I just know it.

You never think it could happen to you. Until one day without warning, it just does...

*   *   *   *   *

...to be continued in TAOC Episodes S1E4

Road to Closure: Episode IV

*Have you ever seen a picture or a portrait –
full of beautiful color and intricate detail, so
complex and deep, and exploding with pure
artistry???? Give it but a glance and you'll never
appreciate the true brilliance behind it.
Yet…stare at it for too long….and you'll
become consumed by its mystique and engrossed
to near obsession.*

Cheating is a work of art.

This…

*…is the masterpiece that I've always liked to
call…*

The Art of Cheating

1

December 2003

The highway ahead was blurry. I was seeing double vision and the yellow lane markings on the road were hopping all over the place. I was almost sure the car wasn't swerving...but I can't say for sure. I can't say I cared. If a highway patrol car got behind me right now...I'd go to jail tonight after they caught me for trying to evade the cops. I was pissy drunk and searching for more intoxication as I chugged big gulps of *Seagram's Gin* right out the pint-sized bottle. My face screwed up while the liquor burned my throat and chest on the way down.

I was going 93 mph now. Flying east down *Highway 50*...in an emotional rage. I had to get back to the Burg as quickly as possible. I was angry, as angry as I had been in a *looooong* time.

Upset. Furious. Ready to snap the fuck out.

The road was empty at the moment...no traffic in front of me. Normally I would be blasting old school rap from my car stereo, but for the 1st time ever, I rode in silence. The wind was gushing hard through the moonroof of my *Honda Accord*...but it did little to help my sweating. My temperature was boiling.

Still, I knew I was making good timing. It had taken me less than 10 minutes to get from the city to *Lee's Summit*, and I was pushing *Annie Mae* to the max. I needed to get there before I was too late...though I wasn't really sure how much time I had honestly.

The phone call that prompted my impromptu return trip home that night was still replaying in my head. Even in my drunken state, I could still remember every word, how careful I was with my questions and assessment of the situation.

My foot pressed hard against the gas pedal...and *Annie Mae* sounded off as she sped up.

I cannot wait 'til I get to the fuckin' Burg!!!!!

I don't know what the fuck I'ma do once I get there...I ain't even thought about it. I ain't thought about shit since I got in the car...not shit else but that phone call.

*   *   *   *   *

"Look, I ain't got no reason to lie about this! I'm just telling you what I heard them saying," the caller said on the other end.

"So it was just *y'all* in the weight room?" I wanted to clarify.

2

"Yeah, like I said," the caller continued. "It was me, *Skates*, and *TJ*. Skates was on the bench and TJ was spotting him."

"I'm saying…maaaan!" I pleaded. "What did this dude *TJ say*?"

"He was telling Skates about how fat *KeLLy's* ass is, and talking 'bout some '*Nigga I was all in dat ish from the back, she was taking it like a pro…*'"

"Man, how you know he was talmbout '*my*' KeLLy?" I asked in doubt.

"Nigga how many thick chicks named *KeLLy* wit a fat ass go to school here?!?!" the caller shot back. "Come on now. You know how niggas talk when they get the pussy…that's what he was on. They probably didn't know I could hear them. I had my earphones on, but they was off. I heard the whole conversation."

"Man look, you bet not be lying about this shit, dude," I warned. "So he said what else?"

"I mean they was just talking about her friends on the *Dance Squad*, saying something about the night they was all playing cards at *TJ's* apartment – cause Skates asked about *Danni*. That's how else I knew they was talking about '*your*' KeLLy – when he said something about *Danni*!"

I started to get antsy as I took it all in, "Man I ain't know that was dude's nickname…that's the only reason I'm kinda believing you. I thought his name was *Marcel*."

3

"That *is* his name...*Marcel* is his government name," they told me. "But all the players on the team and coaches call him *TJ*. Don't ask me where it came from, that's just what we all call him."

"That shit don't even make no sense," I shook my head. "But I guess it does make perfect sense when I think about what happened this morning."

"What happened this morning?" the caller wanted to know.

"Nah, fuck that – so what else he say?" I needed more details. "When he was talking about hitting it from the back?"

"Yeah, you don't like that ish, huh?"

"Don't play with me, yo," I snapped back.

The caller chuckled, "Ok, ok, ok. He was just talking 'bout how she got on top, how he was squeezing her ass and just looking at that mug. I'm guessing she was riding him from the back? That's what it sounded like..."

"This muthafuckin' *bitch!!!* I should drive back down there right now," I contemplated.

"Yo – didn't you say you was drinking?"

"I sure the fuck am!!!" I yelled. "And I'm 'bout to drive my ass back down there *right* now."

4

"No you not! What are you gonna do? It's late and you're *drunk,* Rodney!" they tried to stop me.

"Man I know how to drive! *Fuck* dat! This bitch got me *fucked* up!!" I was fuming. "I'm 'bout to go, I'll holla at you later! Right on."

I dropped my phone to the floor when I said that, unsure if they were still talking on the other end. Sprinting across the room to grab my jacket, I nearly tripped on the long ass phone cord in the middle of the living room floor. I needed to be quiet, so no one would wake up and try to stop me from leaving. My aunt and cousins were all sleeping. I had been in the living room…sipping my drink and watching old episodes of *Martin* when I got the call.

It was late, after midnight. Early December, on a Saturday. I'm almost sure it was the first week of the month. It was chilly outside – but not too cold. Earlier it had rained a light sprinkle, but it wasn't cold enough for anything to stick for the most part. If there wasn't any traffic…I could probably get to the Burg in half the hours' time it usually took. But I need to leave *now*…so I can catch this punk bitch.

She got me fucked up……

*   *   *   *   *

5

2

The sign ahead reads *WARRENSBURG 15 MILES* and I've been in the car about 20 minutes now. It usually takes me 45 minutes or so to get to this point from my aunt's house. I'm not fucking around...

I knew this bitch was up to something. Now it all makes sense – the shit that happened on Thanksgiving, the late-night card games, and what happened this morning. KeLLy is on some sneaky ass *creeping* shit.

This muthafucka!!!

What goes around comes around...or is it what comes around goes around? I don't know what the right way to say it is – it's some bullshit either way if you ask me. I've never believed in karma anyway. But is that what this is?

I CAN'T EVEN THINK STRAIGHT!!!

Ok Rod, get yaself together. KeLLy is cheating on you.

Where did all of this shit start? Shit...I guess it depends on who you ask. One could argue that it started with *my cheating*. If that's the case, then this shit has been a *looooong* time coming. I've had feelings for KeLLy for about two years now…been in love the last year. But I've never been *faithful*. It's weird, I know. But it's the truth from a typical nigga's POV.

KeLLy is my main squeeze, my woman, my lady at home. And I love her to death, but I can't stop cheating. This shit is truly an addiction now. I'll go through spurts sometimes. Weeks…even a couple of months sometimes before I relapse. But hell, I just *can't* stop doing the shit.

And now it's all coming full circle.

Still…fuck that! KeLLy don't get to get no get-back like that. *That's that bullshit.* All men cheat at some point, but don't know nigga wanna see his woman go slut it out for another muhfucka! That's **SCIENCE**. The same is true in my emotional world. I can dish it…but I can't take it.☐ ☐☐

In **HoLLyWorld** though…things are different. In **HoLLyWorld**, we acknowledge the power of *The Art of Cheating*. And in *The Art of Cheating*…there are women playing the game just the same as my fellow men. I gotta remember that at this moment, as I'm flying down the highway to catch Kells.

I'm like a *Master* at this shit. Even when I'm not focused, I'm focused on what I'm not focused on. If KeLLy was out here *cheating* on me…it was only a matter of time before I found out. You can't be better than me at what I do. I put a lot of dedication into this shit, trying to bring balance to living with the *Son's Curse*.

She got me fucked up...

So again...I ask myself, '*Where did all this shit start?*'

See, I been peeping shit for a minute – the last month and a half *in general* been kind of funny.

*   *   *   *   *

Like for instance, Kells and her 'crew' been hanging out a lot more often the second half of this semester. Card games and drinking; girls night out type shit. Ok cool...no big deal, right?

Well one night last month, they were out playing cards the same night I was hanging with some of my frat brothers. One of my bruhs, *Lil Tony*, was a little late getting to the hangout spot, and he pulls me to the side soon as he hits the door, "Yo Nupe, wassup with you and KeLLy?"

"What you mean, Nupe?" I gave him a confused look. "We good! Shit, errthang been cool..."

Lil Tony paused briefly, "Ok, so y'all *are* still together, then. I'm just saying – I was dropping *Kevin* off at *Hawkins*, and I saw her and *Danni* and 'nem walking up the stairs with a couple of basketball players..."

"Yeah, they supposed to be playing cards or some shit," I told him. "One of them lil chicks on the *Dance Squad* live in *Hawkins*."

9

"Yeah, but only reason I'm saying anything is because they all went in *Marcel Martin's* apartment."

"*Marcel Martin?*" I repeated. "Where I know that name from?"

"The point guard from Florida," Lil Tony explained. "He stay two doors down from Kevin's spot."

"Oh…righht right right!" I remembered now. "*Ok.* Hmmm. Yeah, she told me they was going to the one lil bitch she dance with, *Peaches?* Her apartment. But ok. Right on bro. It's all good."

"Y'all already start drinking, yo???" Lil Tony asked as we stepped in the doorway.

"Yeah, *Malone* in there on them drinks now, yo," I replied, trying to hide my discomfort.

That was when I first made a mental note about *Marcel.* There wasn't enough in that intel for me to get real suspicious of KeLLy stepping out. Not at that point. But that was definitely the start to me paying attention…

*   *   *   *   *

I'd kept my cool for a while after that. No probing, no questioning…just keeping my eyes opened. Good thing I did. I can't believe she's really trying to sneak around behind my back. The nerve of this bitch!

If you're gonna cheat…at least play the shit the right

way. KeLLy was *always* telling me shit like this.

She would always say, *"Look Rodney – I know you probably out here still fucking with other bitches. I know **you**. But if you gon do ya dirt – at least don't have that shit all in my face...letting it get back to me! Don't let me find out some shit and not expect me to act a fool!!!"*

And of course, I never shook her hand or *agreed* to the shit...but I always took it literal. I got what she was saying with that shit. Don't have her out here looking stupid when her friends question her about some shit they heard. I can respect that, if for no reason other than me being a student of *The Art* for so long. Hell, that's the first lesson I ever learned. If you're gon do dirt...the least you can do is everything possible in ya power to cover it up.

So why was KeLLy being sloppy? How could she ask that of me...but then I start to find out shit like *this*?!?!

I'ma kill this bitch bro...

*   *   *   *   *

November 2003

A few weeks after the '*card game spotting*', it's Thanksgiving. I'm at KeLLy's parents' and we'd all just finished dinner. So like I said, I'd been keeping my cool. But this night I wasn't so calm. I lost my cool in front of the whole family...but I couldn't help it.

After dinner, I'm sitting in the kitchen as we discuss going to see the Christmas lights on the plaza. KeLLy's mom is sitting next to me. KeLLy is seated next to Miss Fischer, across from me. At the stove stood Kells' younger sister, *Keena*.

"Girl, y'all ain't going nowhere!" she said to Kells. It's already after 8."

"Especially with your boyfriend sitting here sipping his drink," their mama, Miss Fischer chimed in. "You know Rodney, my boyfriend wouldn't have even been drinking in front of my mother before we were married. You should be ashamed."

"Miss Fischer, I'm not being disrespectful," I disagreed. "KeLLy is drinking too!"

"Don't put me in it!!!" KeLLy exclaimed. "Nah brother – you on ya own on this one!"

"Yeah, you know my kids don't show me no type of respect or courtesy either," Miss Fischer shook her head at Keena. "Look at this one – she ain't barely got no darn clothes on and it's *Thanksgiving!*"

"Ooooo Mama – don't do me!" Keena's jaw dropped. "You just gonna dog me out like that – for *RODNEY*!?!"

Just then, KeLLy's cell phone – which was sitting on the table between Mrs. Fischer and I – starts ringing and vibrating. I pick it up to hand it to KeLLy. But as *soon* as I touch it, Kells *jumps* up across the table, moving her mom out the way to reach for the phone, "Gimme my phone Rodney!!!"

What the fuck?!?!

Yeah. It's about to go down.

*　　　*　　　*　　　*　　　*

3

KeLLy damn near knocks her Mom out the chair to reach across her, and I scoot back...out of her reach, "Damn, I was just picking it up to hand it to you! Why you 'bout to jump out ya skin n'stuff???"

Kells stands up and starts walking around the table, "Rodney, give me my phone."

Ok so now I'm more than curious, "No. Why are you acting like that? Whatchu hiding?"

So now me & KeLLy are in a light scuffle. I'm still sitting in the chair playing keep-away, with her trying to reach behind me and get her phone. Now at *first*, I'm just teasing, playing around. But now that we've made eye-contact, I can see that KeLLy is *really* frantically trying to get this damn phone from me. Now I'm suspicious.

"Quit playing, babe," she pleaded softly. "Give it here..."

"Nah, now you got my attention," I refused. "You ain't *never* acted like this over ya phone Kells..."

"How you just gon keep her phone from her like that?" Keena interjected. "*Childish!!!*"

15

I turned my nose up, "This ain't got nothing to do with you, lil girl…"

"Now Rodney, that is '*her*' phone," Miss Fischer spoke up. "You can't do that; you don't pay the bill."

Suddenly I'm feeling outnumbered…which pisses me off. This is where I lose my cool and start raising my voice, "Ok, so *what* I don't pay the bill??? Y'all gon act like y'all ain't see her jump out her *shoes* so I don't see who calling her???"

KeLLy's grabbing my right arm now. Her phone is in my left hand, behind my back. She switches hands, I switch hands. We going back and forth until I stand up, and now my back is against the kitchen wall on the north side of the house. She refuses to give up, "Rodney! GIVE ME MY PHONE!"

"I know y'all better stop playing in my dang kitchen!" Miss Fischer had enough. "Rodney, give her that phone and be done with it! Ain't gon be in here working my nerves over no doggone phone! You give her that phone *right now!*"

Defeated and mad as hell, I finally handed her the phone, "You lucky ya mama right here cuz for real, that's some straight *bull!* Let *me* do something like that and it's *curtains!*"

"Whatever!!" Kells snapped back. "I don't be going through yo phone, and Lord knows what I'll probably find if I did!"

16

"But ain't nobody go through *yo* phone KeLLy!" I pointed out angrily. "So what are you even *talking* about?!?!? Just stop talking to me before I get mad for real. You got ya phone. Leave me alone."

"Ok ok, now calm down Rodney," Miss Fischer stepped in again. "See, that's why you shouldn't drink straight out that bottle like that."

I took a deep breath, trying to show respect, "Miss Fischer, it ain't got nothing to do with the liquor! You just taking up for ya daughter and you know she full of it right now!"

I walked out of the kitchen and into the dark, empty living room…steaming and in disbelief. I know I'm not tripping, but the three of them stay in the kitchen making comments that say otherwise. I let it go, and never bring it up again. For now, I'll just make a mental note.

*   *   *   *   *

December 2003

I've reached Warrensburg city limits now…and I slow down to exit the ramp onto *Highway 13*. I'm low on gas, and the light may come on at any minute, but I'm not stopping for shit. The two-unit duplex where KeLLy and I lived was about seven minutes off the highway. I should make it there in two.

As I make a right turn onto *13*, I start thinking about

the phone call I made sitting in the driveway, right before I left my aunt's earlier.

*   *   *   *   *

I had rushed outside as soon as I got the call about KeLLy. But once I got in the car, I hesitated. I knew all of the shit I'd been hearing and peeping added up to Kells cheating…but still I didn't want to believe it. I sat in the car for about 20 seconds, thinking about all the shit we'd been through. All the times I'd cheated and promised myself it would be the last time. All the times KeLLy had showed how down she was for me, all the love she'd shown me in our short time together. My heart was hurting. I didn't wanna believe it…but I couldn't put it past her. It's not like she was new to this.

I met KeLLy in the fall of 2001, the first semester of my *second* senior year as an undergrad. KeLLy was a 2nd year student and had just transferred from *TSU* that semester. We were from the same city, and her high school friends like *Danni* and *Isha* were already students at CMSU prior to Kells arriving. She also had a boyfriend of 7 years named *Jamal* who was a sophomore on the yard. I didn't let that stop me from trying to holler….and KeLLy didn't let that stop her from hollering back. We creeped for a whole semester and a half before she broke up with *Jamal*….and then we officially became an item in the summer.

KeLLy wuttin' new to this.

In fact, when we were two undergrads creeping, we

18

used to tease each other with our techniques on *cheating* – talking shit about whose strategies were best. I used to help her come up with lies to tell Jamal...and she used to love hearing me make up alibis for my jump-offs on campus, lying in bed with me quiet and giggling. We used to get a rush outta that shit.

Funny how the table turns right?

So, where did all this shit start? Like I said before, depends on who you asking...

I knew KeLLy was a *cheater* in the beginning. She told me she was trying to leave all'at shit behind when I graduated...and so we made somewhat of a mutual pact. I knew I hadn't been able to keep my end of the deal...but this was the first time I suspected KeLLy had relapsed as well.

And the shit *hurt*.

So anyway, back to the call before I left my aunt's. I dialed KeLLy's line...to test the temperature. The phone rang three times. I almost hung up and headed out...but then she picked up. Her voice sounded groggy on the other end, "Helllo?"

"Hello," I said dryly.

"*Rodney*? What time is it? Is everything okay, babe?"

"Yeah, I just needed to hear your voice," I lied. "It sound quiet over there, y'all good?"

19

"Yeah, everybody in the other room sleep," KeLLy lied back. "I was almost knocked out."

"Oh, so y'all all was *sleep*?" I shook my head. "My bad...I ain't mean to wake you, babe. I'll just talk to you tomorrow."

"Are you sure everything is okay, Rodney?" KeLLy tried to probe. "You sound down or something."

"I'm cool, babe," I lied yet again. "I'm 'bout to go to sleep; talk to you tomorrow. Love you."

Kells paused, and I wasn't sure if she yawned or sighed. Then she mumbled, "Ok...I'll call you in the morning when we get up. Love you too...bye."

That '*play sleep*' trick was an old one. KeLLy & I had used it over and over...just not on each other. I could hear it in her voice, something wasn't right. That was all the reassurance I needed (or didn't need) so I hopped right on the road after that...not even stopping to get gas.

I had to get down there while '*everyone was sleep in the other room*' if it killed me...

*   *   *   *   *

4

The Burg was a pretty small town; you could circle the whole city in 45 minutes. The central part of town was all that mattered – the campus and area surrounding it. I had left the Burg after graduation in *2002* and moved back home to KC. KeLLy and I spent that whole summer together, we were literally together every day. That's the first time I can say I truly loved a woman. Any love I had for any female before KeLLy could be considered childhood shit, college included. Shit got real when I met Kells…I realized I had finally met my match.

KeLLy felt the same way about me…we had a strange bond right in the beginning because we were so much alike mentality-wise. Early on in our relationship we were on some *Bonnie & Clyde* shit…two peas in a pod. What started off as purely sexual quickly turned into a real friendship turned lovers. By the end of that summer, we couldn't be separated.

By then it was time for KeLLy to go back to school. And since she hated *CMSU* so much (*she only transferred to be closer to Jamal*), she was headed out of state and back to *TSU*. We cried in each other's arms to sleep the night before she left…and I was shaking in the car on the way back to Missouri, sad and blue.

KeLLy couldn't stay away for long though...and ended up coming back home mid-semester. She took a year off and naturally, with her back home, we grew even closer.

When she got ready to go back to school again, it wasn't going to be out-of-state...because *wherever* she was going, I was going with her.

We prolly shoulda never came back to the Burg together. The Burg was where it all began for two *cheaters* who found love. We shoulda never looked back. We shoulda never fuckin' came back here...

The duplex where KeLLy and I lived was one block from campus. You could walk through a field and be behind *Hawkins* – the upperclassman apartments on campus. My first destination was our spot.

As I stopped at the corner before our block, I felt a lump in my throat. I had no idea what I was bound to see...no clue or preparation for what may be discovered after this night. This is the first time anything like this has ever happened to me. I've never felt this feeling of anxiety and insecurity – this is foreign territory for me.

I put the car in Park, feeling hesitant. Maybe I should just turn around.

I wish I could go back to this morning....

*   *   *   *   *

KeLLy woke up after I did…she lifted her head up off my chest around 8:30am. I had been up since 8, staring at the ceiling. For some reason, I woke up that morning homesick. I missed my family. I hadn't been home since Thanksgiving, and even then, I spent most of my holiday with KeLLy's family. As soon as Kelly looked up and saw me, she could sense that I was feeling down, "Baby what's wrong? Are you hungry?"

I chuckled, "I am hungry, but that's not what's wrong…"

"What's wrong then?" she smiled at me. "Good morning."

Kells curled her right leg up on mine…brushing my semi-hard dick as she snuggled up to me. "Oh *that's* what's wrong – nasty!" she licked her teeth. "You want some morning sex, honey?"

She reached under the sheets…but I pushed her hand away, "No Kells…stop it. I am hungry though…"

I bit my lip, and she lowered her eyes, "*That kind of hungry??*"

"NO!!" I yelled. That's definitely not what I meant.

"Well, boy I'm confused!" she pulled away. "Hell…you say you hungry but that ain't what's wrong. You say you don't want no pussy…well what do you want me to do Rodney???"

I snatched her back towards me, "Who you talking to like that?"

"Don't be grabbing me like that! You know I like that rough stuff," she warned. "I'm talking to *you*, nigga – who else in the room?"

*Now I **am** getting kind of horny.*

"You want me to rough you up, girl?" I asked mischievously.

"I want you to tell me what's wrong. For real," Kells said with concern.

So I start talking to Kells, like I always do. She knows me like a book anyway. She can tell when something is bothering me – she's very in tune with my emotions. That's why it's very important to be mindful of everything I do in regards to *The Art of Cheating* because, if some shit is off, KeLLy will notice.

That morning, I told her about how I was missing my family…how I was struggling with not being able to be away for too long. How my family thought I never spent enough time with them when I was in KC, and how they were probably right. And then we talked about how I much I loved just being away with her…how she was the perfect getaway from all the drama at home in my world. KeLLy then related to it…sharing the same thought and emotion as it pertained to her being homesick and missing her own family. We shared a real moment.

"Well baby…maybe you should go home and visit your family tonight," she suggested. "You don't have to work 'til Monday, and it'll be good."

"I thought you was braiding *Peaches'* hair today. Nah that ain't gon work Kells."

"Yes, I'm braiding *Peaches'* hair at 9. What time is it?" she looked at the clock. "No…I meant you can go to KC without me. It'll be good to be around your people with just '*you*' – ya know? I'm always with you, babe. Y'all gotta bond sometime, too! Hell, I'm sure yo family get tired of me around all the time anyway…"

"I mean, it ain't even like that," I shook my head at her.

"Well, regardless of that…you should go.," Kells insisted. "You getting kicked out anyway, cuz the girls having a slumber party here tonight."

"That's tonight??" I was taken aback. "Damn, today *is* Saturday…that's right. Well damn…where was you gonna send me?!?!?"

KeLLy laughed sarcastically, "Shit, I'm sure one of yo bruhs will let you get pissy drunk and pass out on the floor like you like to do these days. Don't act brand new…"

"Damn, it's like that?" I reached under the covers for her chocolate nipple….and she knocked my hand away.

27

"Stop, Rodney!" she cried. "I gotta get up before Peaches and 'nem get here! No!"

"Come on...they ain't even here," I whispered. "All I need is like 3 minu..."

Before I could finish, the doorbell rang. KeLLy hopped up – tossing the sheets on me and in my face. Her dark and thick ass cheeks dribbled as she pranced toward her robe.

"See that's that *buuuullllllllshit*," I sunk back in the bed.

"Welp...sorry for ya!" her hard laughing echoed throughout the hallway.

She hurried to the living room to let her friends in and I got up to get ready to shower. There's no way I was sticking around here with all them heffas coming over again. That trip home alone just might be the best move.

As I slipped my gym shorts on...KeLLy's phone started ringing on the end table next to our queen size bed. I heard it ring, I looked at it vibrate...but I didn't pick it up.

"KeLLy!!! Ya phone ringing!!!"

She was in the front room, and I could hear all them skanks coming in way too hyper for it to be so early. Danni's voice was the loudest, as always.

"Just answer it!" Kells yelled above their voices.

"Girl, I am not answering yo phone!" I screamed back. "I ain't even touching it."

"Rodney, answer the phone!"

I pick it up off the table, but it stops ringing. There's a missed call from a *660-area code*. Warrensburg number. I start to walk through the hallway…to take KeLLy her phone. Once I turn the corner, it starts ringing again.

My living room is filled with all the *Dance Squad* girls…half of them at least. Kells is in her chair across the room, going through bags of hair already. She looks up briefly but doesn't move otherwise, "Answer it, Rodney. See who it is…"

Ok fine. I'll answer. It's the same number — somebody here in the Burg.

"Hello?" I flipped open the Sprint cell phone.

"Hello, can I speak to KeLLy?" said the deep voice on the other end.

"Uhhh…yes, may I ask who's calling?" I responded with courtesy.

"Yeah. This *TJ*…"

*   *   *   *   *

5

"Ok, hold on," I handed her the phone, told her who it was, then headed for the shower. I didn't flinch or even raise an *eyebrow* when I heard the male voice on the other end. KeLLy has a cousin named *TJ*. No big deal.

*   *   *   *   *

Except now that I was back in the Burg at nearly 1 in the morning, *everything* about this morning was a big deal. The way KeLLy had talked me into leaving so she could have the house to herself. How she had used the slumber party as a coverup – she had told me about the *Dance Squad* slumber party *weeks* ago, like *before* Thanksgiving. How she ain't wanna have sex *all of a sudden*…and then this guy *TJ* called.

This morning…I automatically assumed it was her *cousin* TJ calling. I mean, it all made sense. Why would she tell me to answer her phone if some other nigga was calling her – after our big fight on Thanksgiving? I just knew it was her cousin. KeLLy's cousins visit her in the Burg often…it wouldn't have been far-fetched if her cousin TJ was calling her from somewhere in the Burg on a Saturday morning.

31

KeLLy knew all of this. She knew I would assume it was cousin TJ and *not trip*. She knew my tendencies, what I was likely to question or lose my cool about. She was this good at *The Art of Cheating*, I had to remember this. We once played by the same rules.

This punk ass bitch….

You can never be better than a *Master* at this shit. And honestly at this point in **HoLLyHistory,** maybe I wasn't a Master just yet. But I was most definitely a *Jedi*…and KeLLy was nothing more than one who was strong in abilities. She didn't take this shit as serious as I did anymore. I was ready for the Master trials, and she wasn't on my level. That's why she got sloppy. That **'table hop for the phone'** was *the* slip-up…that was the trigger for me. Had I not witnessed her act out of character in that one defining moment – my bell may have never been rung.

Still. This morning, when I heard the name TJ, the alarm wasn't sounding off completely.

It was the call I got nearly two hours ago…when I found out that TJ was also the nickname of *Marcel Martin*, the starting point guard from Florida that played for the basketball team. The *same* Marcel who KeLLy was spotted with by my frat brother, *Lil Tony*, along with her crew, going into his apartment for a card night that I was told was hosted by *Peaches*.

Marcel Martin *is* TJ. And TJ was in the weight room talking to niggaz about hitting my girl from the back!!!

32

LAWD!!!!!!!

Now the tears are rolling.

Get yourself together, Rod. You gotta follow through.

    *   *   *   *   *

I crack my knuckles and proceed past the stop sign, driving slowly down the dim-lit street before turning my headlights off. Our house was the 3rd down on my left. Upon approaching, the first thing I noticed was that all the lights were off inside. Maybe they *are* having a slumber party.

But then as I get closer, I see the driveway empty…there isn't a single car parked anywhere near our building.

Hmmm.

I don't stop. Instead, I keep driving 'til I get to the end of the block, hanging a left and a quick right. I park the car near the baseball field and start walking back towards the house. I'm wearing a dark blue hoodie sweat suit, my *First Down* jacket still in the car. It's cold as fuck, but my adrenaline is running and I'm drunk. I almost trip on a sewer hole as I cross the street.

My walk ended up being a waste of time – no one was home. I circled the house twice, walked up on the windows, and listened. Our bedroom had windows on two sides, and the one on the backside was eye-level. The entire house was pitch black dark and quiet. No cars – not even KeLLy's – were in sight. Wuttin' no way they had a slumber party going on, so I unlocked the front door without fear of startling any sleeping bitches.

The place was empty and a mess. I could tell that KeLLy and the girls had partied all day…but *now*, they were all gone.

I walked back to my car and sat for a few minutes, warming up.

It had taken me about 28 minutes to get to the Burg after pulling out of my aunt's driveway. KeLLy said everyone was at the house sleep about 40 minutes ago. She was riding with that '*slumber party*' alibi 'til the wheels fell off. I was impressed. But the wheels was coming the fuck off tonight…fuck that.

I need to find her ass…right fuckin' now. She got me fucked up.

Less than a minute later, I'm flying back up our street and speeding past the house. I make a right at the corner and drive down the slight hill towards *Hawkins Apartments* to my right. I drive to the end of the street, noting that the entire parking lot is empty except for two cars.

KeLLy's car is on the bottom end. I make a right and then another right into the lot, peeling through it past her car and back out the exit uphill.

I'm fuming mad now. I make a left back onto our street and drive back down the block…staring in a daze.

34

My heart is racing.

I find myself circling the block and coming back up on *Hawkins* from the other end this time. I stop in the middle of the street, behind the building. The pint of gin is nearly gone, less than a third is swirling around in the bottom of the bottle. I take another shot to the head. My flip phone is in my hand seconds later…dialing KeLLy.

It rings.

And rings.

My heart beats louder.

It rings. And rings again.

My heart is thumping. I'm breathing heavily.

It's still ringing.

My eyes are closed.

Her voice mail picks up…

The world goes silent.

I sit still. Very still. I only hear the roar of my engine running. I don't even hear myself breathing. Am I breathing?

PHONE RINGS

And all I can do is stare at it for a second before it wakes me up out of my trance. I answer KeLLy's call without clearing my groggy throat, "Hello...?"

"Rodney? Did you just call?" she whispered.

"Yea, I'm sorry I woke you up, babe," I told her. "You at home?"

"Yeah, I'm at home," Kells lied once more. "Are you ok?"

I go silent. She's clearing her throat...but I don't say a word.

"Hello?" she asked, checking to see if I'm still there.

"Huh, babe?"

KeLLy clears her throat again, "I said...yes, I'm home and are you OK???"

SHE. GOT. ME. FUCKED. UP.

*   *   *   *   *

6

My first instinct is to snap out.

I *know* she's not home. I wanna scream and yell…but all that comes out is somewhat of a whimper, "Ooh…ok."

"You sound like you been drinking," she wondered. "Are you *drunk*?"

"I'm cool" I sighed. "I'll call you in the morning, babe. Go back to sleep."

She didn't protest and hurried off the phone. I sat there for a couple of seconds before I snapped back to life and floored the gas pedal. The apartment building flew past the corner of my eye and I coughed loudly before bringing the car to a screeching halt.

I'm 'bout to go up to dis nigga's apartment and drag her up outta der!!! Soon as I figure out which one is his.

*   *   *   *   *

I remembered Lil Tony said that TJ stayed a couple doors down from his homeboy *Kevin*. Or maybe he said *a*

39

few doors down. Whatever.

It was **1:13am** now, and I was dialing Lil Tony's cell phone. I figured he might be still out kicking it downtown. On a Saturday in the Burg, downtown was the place to be. But Lil Tony would at least know which unit belonged to this old hooping ass TJ nigga.

I'ma flip when I figure this out. Tony's phone rang twice before going to his voicemail, so I was shit outta luck there.

And I ain't have the *slightest* idea which apartment could be TJ's. This was his first year at the school and I was barely on campus anymore. I was only taking three grad classes, with two of them being night classes. I ain't know who was who anymore…and there was over 100 units in the *Hawkins* building. It wouldn't make no sense to just start *guessing*.

Now all of a sudden, I was feeling defeated. I had about a half-second urge to throw a brick through her car window…but that just felt like some bitch shit, so I shrugged it off quickly.

Suddenly, it came to me. I sped off the other way – away from *Hawkins* and away from campus. Suddenly, I had an idea.

*　　*　　*　　*　　*

I ended up about 5 minutes from campus, close to downtown Warrensburg….at another off-campus apartment complex. I hopped out the car immediately and ran up the stairs in the back of the building. I found myself bent over, gasping for air once reaching the top of the stairs. After about 10 seconds, I gathered the energy to beat on the wooden door until *J Dub* opened up.

J Dub was my frat brother and *ship* – meaning we pledged on the same line. I knew he'd be up, he worked at the bowling alley that closed at midnight. His shift usually ended between 12:45am and 1am…and he had just microwaved dinner. Surprised to see me so late, J Dub embraced me and let me right in, "What – you locked out the house, bro?"

"Bro, you wouldn't believe the type of night I'm having," I shook my head at him. So I fill my frat in, telling him how I put all the clues together and now all I need to find out is which unit this dude TJ stayed in. J Dub couldn't get past Marcel's nickname being '*TJ*'.

"Are you sure that's dude's name though, Rod?" my ship asked curiously. "And he don't even seem like KeLLy's *type* for real…"

"Nigga, her last dude was that short, funny looking nigga – what the fuck *is* her type?" I snapped back. "Man, I'm sure about the nickname, ship. *Now* I'm 100% sure. The whole team calls that nigga *TJ*."

I sat down at J Dub's computer and moved the mouse. "Are you online?" I asked, clicking around on the screen.

"Yeah, click that *AOL* icon on the desktop," J-Dub advised.

As I pull up the internet and the *Mules Basketball* home page, I keep talking…burping in between breaths, "Yeah, see I'm just going off what I heard. Lil Tony saw this nigga going in his crib with her, it's gotta be the same person."

"But why '*TJ*' though Rod?" J-Dub tried to make sense of it. "Shouldn't his nickname be *M&M* or some shit Nupe?"

"Nigga, you would think, right?" I agreed. "Man, I don't know. I'm trying to pull up his bio on the team page…"

Who remembers high-speed dialup? Well…yeah. Five minutes later, the page was finally fully loaded and me and J Dub sat staring at the team picture. Sure enough, they've got #30 listed as *Marcel Martin* out of Tallahassee, FL. But no mention of '*TJ*'. We keep scrolling, until we get to the roster, where each player had an individual bio with a backstory.

Martin's backstory was pretty interesting. This guy was all-state and didn't play 4 full years in high school. He had a rep for his lightening quick first step and fearlessness going to the hole. But his biggest bullet point fell right in line with what I needed to find out. At the very bottom of the page, it talked about how the kids in his neighborhood started calling him '*TJ*'…which stood for '*that jumper*'.

42

BINGO!

"BAM! There it is!" I exclaimed. "Told you!"

"Ok, so it *is* the same nigga," J-Dub stared in disbelief. "Now what?"

"Now I go back to the *Central* home page…and find him in the student directory," I replied with certainty. "Easy!"

"Nigga, you know *Central* ain't that advanced yet," J-Dub chuckled. "Here, lemme find the campus white pages, that shit ain't gon be online."

My ship then goes in the living room of his two-bedroom apartment and comes back with the burgundy paperback directory. I turn right to the M's and start squinting down at the names.

"Nigga, where yo glasses at?" J-Dub noticed me straining my eyes.

"Bro, you know I hate wearing them shits…"

J-Dub paused, "Wait a minute, Rod…how can you see at night when you driving without them?"

"I can't," I admitted as I found what I was looking for. "Ok, it's two *'Marcel Martins'* that go here. Wow."

"Oh, for real???" he sounded surprised.

43

"Yup. But only one in *Hawkins*," I said victoriously. "3A – got it!"

"You got it?!?!" J-Dub's eyes lit up. "Oh shit."

I'm already looking for my keys…and quickly discover them in my pocket. I can't even breathe right now, I'm so ready. "I need to get back over there before she figure out I'm down here," I urged, heading for the door.

"Rod – *wait* a minute. You don't need to be driving," he stopped me. "Come on, I'll take you back over there, ship. Lemme find my sweats."

*   *   *   *   *

Less than 3 minutes later, I'm in the passenger seat to J Dub's '99 *Altima*…shaking like I'm freezing, yet I'm boiling hot. I can't believe all this shit is happening…I feel so betrayed. It's like I've forgotten about all the times I've stepped out on KeLLy – the dynamic of everything changes now. I can't get over the mere thought of another nigga touching her the way I do…kissing her body all over like I love to do so much.

How could she do this to us??? I'ma end up in jail tonight.

J Dub finally pulls up and parks next to KeLLy's car. We sit there for a second as he turns the engine and headlights off.

"Yea, see I told you, her car right there," I pointed

44

out. "Gon tell me they having a slumber party!!! See – all them hoes in on it."

"Aight, we here now," J-Dub sat back. "Whatchu wanna do, Rod?"

"Lemme *call* her again. Hold on."

This time I call back-to-back-to-back. No answer. I start tapping my foot, getting more upset, "See, now this bitch don't wanna answer the phone…"

"You think she know we here?" my ship wondered.

"Nah…lemme try one more time."

When I call back this time…KeLLy picks right up, "Hello? Rodney, what is going *on*?"

"Oh, you *up* now?" I was hyper and antsy. "Where you *at* Kelly?"

KeLLy paused, assessing my energy, "I told you where I was Rodney. I'm at home."

"You at home?" I snarled. "That's funny…cuz I'm sitting here looking at yo car. And yo *car* ain't at home…"

"Huh?" her voice wavered.

"*Huh???*" I repeated sarcastically.

KeLLy paused again, longer this time, "What are you

45

talking about? Where are you?"

"I just *told* you," I reiterated. "I'm outside, *next* to yo car....and it's not at the house."

I hear a long silence...and then nothing. Not even breathing or static on the other line.

"Hello????"

"I'm here," KeLLy finally responds. "I don't know what you talking about though, Rodney. I'm at *home*. It's late...I'ma call you in the morning."

"KeLLy, don't hang up this phone," I yelled quickly.

The call is disconnected suddenly. I look at J Dub...and he's got this look of worry on his face. He already knows what I'm thinking when I hop out the car. I start making a dash for the stairway on the side of *Hawkins*, teeth clenched...fists balled up.

I can't take this shit no more!!!

I'm at 3A within seconds. It's the first door on the end of the third floor, on the side of the building where KeLLy's car is parked. Now I'm banging on the door with my right fist...each pound harder than the one before...

*　　　*　　　*　　　*　　　*

7

I'm banging for about ten seconds straight. And I mean I'm beating this door *in* with it. It's a metal door, like them cheap motel joints. But the force of my super-knock is moving the door slightly…I could probably kick it in if I wanted to. I pause momentarily, looking at the door to make sure it was the right one.

What's taking them so long to answer? I'm not going away.

After about a minute or so, I hear him on the other side of the door…voice pitch low, "Who is it???"

"It's Rodney. Open the door, bro."

Silence.

And then more silence.

What the fuck?!?!?

I start banging on the door again like a madman.

This lil hoe ass nigga need to open this door before I start kicking!!!

Ironically, he then snatches the door open at that thought. He's shorter than me...*how the fuck he hooping for the school and he's an inch shorter than me?* But it's definitely the same guy from the web page...brown-skinned, skinny nigga with a short fade. He's wearing a pair of his *Mules* shorts and a white wife beater. His eyes are bloodshot red...and I can't tell if he's been sleep or just high. KeLLy hates being around me when I smoke....so she better not be ok with this little fuck blowing around her. The very *thought* just pisses me off even more.

"Maaaaan...*wassup* bro?" TJ stood there tight-lipped. "Why you knocking on my door like dat this late, *blood*?"

He's standing in the doorway, and all I see is pitch black behind him.

"Yeah, I ain't mean to wake you up, bro," I spoke calmly. "Where *KeLLy*?"

"KeLLy?" he played dumb. "Ain't no *KeLLy* here, bruh..."

My eyebrow raised and I gave him a little smirk, "KeLLy's not here?!?"

I look to my left and see J Dub finally making it up the stairs, he's taking his time. TJ glances at him, eyes cutting to his right, "Nah bro, ain't no KeLLy here..."

"Nigga," I tried to reason with him. "You *sure*?!?!?

50

Her car right there..."

"Nah bruh, KeLLy ain't here," TJ stuck to his statement.

I started shaking my head, feeling my breathing intensify, "Bruh...I'm almost *sure* she in there. Do you know who KeLLy is?"

Yeah, I know who you talmbout, blood. She on the *Dance* team," his voice remains nonchalant.

"And she ain't in there?"

TJ chuckled, "Nah bruh, she not hea..."

"Has she *ever* been over here??" I asked, paying close attention to all his body language. I bit my lip.

"Nah bruh," he repeated. "She ain't never been over hea, bruh."

"Man, you lying, bro!" I shouted. "I *know* she in there!!"

I step in, and TJ steps out further...closer to me. We're right in each other's grill. I start to take another step closer, but my ship's voice stops me, "Rod. He say she ain't here, Nupe."

I'm not ready to give up...

"Nah man, he lying," I told J Dub. "I know dat bitch

51

in here."

J Dub grabs me by my right arm, pulling me away. Me and TJ's eyes stay locked. His jaws are tightening up.

"I ain't got no reason to lie to you, bruh bruh," he said without budging.

"Come on, Rod…it ain't on him," J Dub insisted.

It takes me a second, but I finally stop resisting J Dub and start walking away with him. I'm cussing like a sailor on the way back down to the car, and not planning on leaving anytime soon. We get back to the parked cars and I sit on her hood…smashing it in with my weight.

"I know she in there, Nupe…"

J Dub shook his head, "Man, we can't just run up in dude crib. He say she ain't in there, what we supposed to do?"

This was one of those moments where I appreciated the techniques of some of my hood comrades from back home over my college buddies.

"Man, I don't know. I ain't leaving 'til she come out though, bro," I stood my ground, fully prepared for an all-nighter.

J Dub let out a deep sigh, "Well nigga, I'm sitting in the car. It's cold out here – shit."

As Dub got in his car, I pulled out my phone...still sitting firmly on KeLLy's *Kia*. She picked up on the first ring, "Yes, Rodney..."

"Where you at, KeLLy?" my tone was direct and impatient.

"You know where I am, Rodney," Kells replied softly. "You out by my car."

"So why that bitch ass nigga say you ain't in there? You damn right I know where yo *lying* ass at!"

"Don't start yelling, Rodney. *I* told him to say I wasn't here! You was beating on the door like the police in the middle of the night!" she cried out.

I raised my voice even more, "Man I wouldn't give a fu – KeLLy, bring yo ass on out here."

"No."

"The fuck you mean – no?!?!" I yelled in shock. "Girl you better bring yo *muthafuckin* ass out here right muthafuckin *now*!!!"

"No, Rodney...I don't know what you're gonna do to me," she sounded afraid. "You been drinking, you yelling..."

"So fucking *what*?!?! You better bring yo ass out

here!"

"No, I'm *scared* Rodney," she said. "Listen to you…"

I rolled my eyes, "Maaan, I ain't 'bout to put my hands on you. Bring ya ass."

"Then, what are you gonna do?" Kells wanted to know.

"You better bring yo ass KeLLy," I told her with finality.

Kells paused, "Hmmm…no. I don't feel comfortable. I'm not coming out."

"You don't feel *comfortable*?!?!?!" I'm screaming at the top of my lungs now. "Who gives a flying fuck how *YOU* feel right now?!?! Got me out here in the cold running all over town in the middle of the fuckin *night!!!* Bring yo *PUNK* ass out here and face the muthafuckin' *MUSIC!!!*"

J Dub sees me getting hype on the phone and opens up his door, sticking one leg out.

"For real…I'm not playing with you KeLLy," I continued. "Bring yo ass………hello? *HELLO*?!?!?!"

This bitch done hung up on me…

I'm starting to see red. I take off for the stairs again…and I hear J Dub screaming my name behind me…but I'm already past the second floor. I'm at TJ's door again in seconds…banging with the same fist.

This time, he doesn't hesitate to answer. He swings the door open, face frowned up…still pitch black on the inside behind him, "Bro, come on with dat shit…banging on my doe like dat!"

"Man, tell her to bring her ass out here bro," I made myself clear. I'm done playing games.

"Man wassup, bro??" TJ barked at me. "You over hea banging on my doe, got ya homeboy wit you n'shit…"

"Nigga, I ain't got no beef with you…this ain't got shit to do witchu! My nigga just drove me over here. Just tell her to bring her ass, nigga…"

At this point, I see two other cats coming from the other end of the balcony…and J Dub is opposite side, at the stairway I just ran up. As the other guys get closer, I see it's one of the cats from the basketball team…and this other young cat I recognized from KC. I think his came was *Chad* – he was a freshman that year.

So Chad and the other *hooper cat* come down where we all standing in front of the door. TJ feels a lot more comfortable now, and he steps outside the doorway.

"Wassup, cuzz?" Chad peeped the scene. "What's the word?"

I frowned at TJ, "What? You called ya lil homies, bruh?"

The Hooper Cat steps in between me and TJ, facing him, "You good, bro?"

TJ doesn't say a word, instead he steps to the side and the *Hooper Cat* walked in his apartment into the darkness. J Dub moves to his right and starts talking to Chad.

"Bro, you ova hea knocking like the *police*! My niggaz just making sure everything good," TJ said, staring me down again.

I didn't flinch, "I told you it's all good, bro! Tell her to bring her ass out here, nigga! I'm not leaving 'til she come outside."

"Rod, come on…we gon wait downstairs for her. You waking up this nigga's neighbors," J Dub shot me a look. "Aye Lil Chad, we downstairs bro. Come on Rod."

"Man, dis dat bullshit, bro!" I let out a deep sigh.

"Come on Nupe," he ignored my obvious frustration as he waited for me to walk away.

So now I'm *back* downstairs with J Dub. He's standing next to the cars and I'm sitting on her hood once more. I call KeLLy's phone again….no answer. After about five more minutes, Chad and Hooper Cat come back downstairs, and TJ is standing on the balcony overlooking the almost empty parking lot.

Lil Chad approached me slowly and peacefully, "Aye

Rod, wassup cuzz – holla at me. You know I know you from the town…and this my nigga upstairs. She scared, thinking you bout to beat her ass. Let me know what's good…"

"Cuzz, I don't even know why he called y'all," I told him before thinking about it. "I mean, I *was* banging on his shit. I'm mad as a muhfucka but I ain't got no beef with *him,* bro. I told him that. I don't know why he think we tripping – I just want my girl to come outside. I'm not finna nothing to her, bro."

Chad looks at Hooper Cat and shrugs his shoulders, "Aye, he said he just want his girl to come out…that's it. You gotta respect that. Aight, I'ma go talk to her, bro."

They walk off and head back upstairs. J Dub is looking at me, searching for some sort of sign, "Rod, you ain't gon snap out – right?"

"I'm cool, ship," I mumbled under my breath.

"ROD!" he raised his voice.

"Bro, I'm good," I reassured him, being honest. "She just need to come on outside, so we can go home and hash this shit out. I'm not gon snap, bro."

My eyes are locked on the balcony, and TJ and Hooper Cat are standing outside his door…talking. Chad is nowhere to be seen so I assume he's in the apartment, talking to KeLLy.

About a minute or so later...KeLLy comes walking out the apartment, with a small bag over her shoulder. Her overnight bag.

My hand starts shaking and I bite my lip hard.

I can't wait 'til she gets downstairs...

*   *   *   *   *

8

She walks down the stairs slowly. I can hear her keys jingling as she nears the bottom. I chew on my lip, my heart racing.

Keep your cool Rod.

J Dub is watching me closely, ready to break it up if it gets physical.

But he ain't got nothing to worry about. Once she circled the stairway corner and stepped out into the light...I froze up. KeLLy looked almost like she was glowing...and I remembered why I was so caught up in the first place. Even in her cheating, conniving moment...KeLLy had me open.

She was everything physically my type. Child-bearing hips and thick...her ass was just right. Not small by any means...but not a juggernaut either. Just right. Her skin...a deep, smooth chocolate tint....no blemishes. She rarely wore weave...almost never. She hated it...she used to talk about how all the chicks I messed with before her were weave-heads. Tonight was no different, KeLLy wore her hair straightened and down to her shoulders...strands blowing in the wind covering the right side of her face as she approached us. She didn't look up until she was right in our faces...big and round brown eyes watering, "Hey Jamie."

She shivered as she spoke softly, and her puffy, baby face jaws were trembling. She didn't look my way. I was glaring at her...wishing she glanced at me so I could spit at her...but knowing if she made eye contact, I would soften up. Good thing she ain't know that. KeLLy was terrified, and I could smell her fear. I just hoped she couldn't smell my vulnerability. Deep down inside...and I wasn't sure if anyone could tell...but deep down I felt so fucking weak. So defeated.

"Well, hello, KeLLy," J Dub spoke back to her.

"Come on, take me back to my car," I said, talking to Kells.

"Rod...are you cool?" J Dub checked my temperature yet again.

"I'm cool bro. I'ma ride with her back to yo spot and get my car so I can get my shit from her crib."

"Rod," he wasn't convinced. "Are you cool, though???"

"Come on KeLLy," I'm already standing at her passenger side door. "Nupe, I'm cool."

She turns around slowly but moves quickly to the other side. She still ain't looked at me. J Dub walks over to me and grips me up, whispering , "Bro, don't do nothing stupid. Put it on the Bond you won't, bro."

"Maaan," I halfway pouted. "Come on, ship…"

"*On the Bond,* Rod?" he pressed on.

I shook my head, "*On the Bond,* bro. I'm going to get my shit…I'm coming back to yo spot."

He's finally convinced, and lets my hand go. Without another moment's hesitation, I open the passenger door. KeLLy's started the car, and I'll be damned if this bitch drives off without me.

*　　*　　*　　*　　*

"So you just not gon say shit?" hoarse, my voice was barely above a whisper. She's staring into space ahead, and I'm staring at her.

"What do you want me to say, Rodney?" she muttered.

"I want you to say *something*!"

KeLLy paused, "I mean…I don't *know* what I'm supposed to say, Rodney."

I started getting animated, and yelled, "Fuck what's '*supposed*' to happen!! Obviously, we waaaaay past that point! *Fuck* that!! You need to tell me what the fuck!?!?"

63

"Rodney, you're scaring me when you yell and curse like that."

"*Maaaaan* fuck that!" I screamed angrily.

"Please calm down, babe," she pleaded with me, making it worse.

"Don't call me *that!!*" I snapped. "And how the fuck – *maaaan* how the *FUCK* you gon tell me to *calm* down?!!? What kinda shit is that to say right now?!?! *NO* I'm not finna fuckin *calm down* KeLLy – I just caught yo ass *cheating* on me!"

Her voice wavered, "Rodney, please. You have to stop curs…."

"Maaan aight," I cut her off, realizing what was going on. "You tryna stall time n'shit, like you ain't never heard a nigga *curse!* You on some muthafuckin' *bullshit,* up there laid up with some nigga getting yo back blown out. *You got me fucked up…*"

"Ain't nobody get they back blown out…"

"Oh – but you heard *that* through the *cursing,* huh?!" I pointed out. "Yeah, that's ok, wait 'til we get to the house."

"What's gonna happen when we get home, Rodney?" she asked nervously.

I turned away and looked out the window, "We gon

talk."

The rest of the way to J Dub's, we ride in silence. I finally get back in my car and start to trail behind her. She's driving slowly, still trying to stall time n'shit. My heart is pounding...I need to hear some music or something. Hitting the power button on my deck, sounds of *Dr. Dre's* album *'The Chronic'* hit my ears. Perfect.

Track 16 on REPEAT.

*   *   *   *   *

I'm scrambling all through the house now, grabbing my possessions from every corner...stuffing shit in trash bags. KeLLy is following me every step of the way and pleading with me, "Rodney, where are you gonna go?"

"I don't know," I kept moving. "Why you even care? Quit talking to me, man."

"I thought we were gonna talk," she reminded me.

I rolled my eyes, "For real, what's there to talk about? It's all out in the open now..."

"Is it?" her voice had a hint of sarcasm.

"I mean – you caught!" I shot back. "I caught you...red fuckin' handed."

"What did you catch me doing, Rodney?" she challenged slyly.

"Ok see, I'm not 'bout to play with you," I told her sternly. "Just stop fuckin *talking* to me!!"

"No, I'm asking. Let's put it all out in the open for real," she suggested. "Ok, so I was spending the night over *TJ's*. Let's talk about it."

I thought she was bat shit crazy, shaking my head, "KeLLy, move the fuck out my way before I slap the dog shit outta you, for real."

She stepped in my path and looked deeply in my eyes, "You wanna *slap* me now, Rodney?"

"Move."

"Go 'head…slap me!" she stuck her face out. "That's gonna make you feel better?"

"Nah, what's gon make me feel better is if I just get the fuck *away* from you as quick as possible," I stepped around her quickly, "I can't even *look* at you right now."

"Babe, let's talk," she spoke softly again, getting further under my skin.

"Quit *CALLING* me that shit!" I snapped at her. "I'm not yo *babe*…"

"Yes, you are, babe. Don't say that," she frowned. "I'm sorry you *hurt,* Rodney. I'm sorry I hurt you." She follows me back into the bedroom and stands in the doorway to block me from going back up front.

"You not sorry. You sorry you got *caught*."

"Rodney, I *am* sorry that I hurt you. I am," she insisted.

"Fuck you," I replied harshly.

Silence.

"Wow," she looked surprised. "You never say that to me."

"I can't believe you did this, KeLLy," my voice cracked.

She sees the tears forming in my eyes and starts towards me, reaching out. I slap her hand away.

"Baby…can we talk about this?" she asked again. "Please…"

"No…leave me be."

"Rodney, I can't," she claimed. "We have to talk about this."

I'm wiping my eyes…fighting the tears, "Why? Nah fuck that…I need to *go*. Move out my way."

She doesn't budge, "No, we need to talk."

"About whaaat???!?!?!" I yelled in an emotional whine.

"*Everything.* For *one*...you think I had sex with him. And I *didn't.*"

* * * * *

9

I try to swallow, but there's that lump in my throat again, "Man, shut the fuck up. You think I'm 'bout to believe dat shit? *Yeah right*."

I mean, this bitch been creeping with this nigga at least since Thanksgiving – ain't no *way* she ain't gave this nigga the pussy. Not that it mattered. She was spending the *night* with this nigga...it ain't matter if she fucked him yet or not.

Except...it did.

I hated to say it...but that shit *did* kind of matter from my point of view at the time. More *Art of Cheating* principles. From a *cheater's* standpoint...it's all about the *level* of the *cheating*.

How can a man *cheat* on a woman and justify it? How can I say I love KeLLy...after all the other random pussy I've been getting? But see...that's all it is to a man, though...just pussy. If he following the rules, all a man is tryna do with his side piece is just *fuck*. It's worse if he starts to develop feelings for the other chicks. If he start tricking off his time and money...then that's just taking it too damn far! That's the cardinal sin in **The Art**.

I can look myself in the mirror...and KeLLy in the eye...because I know I had nothing of substance with anybody else. If I'm cheating on my girl, I'm not cheating on her emotionally. And damn sure not financially. A cheating man truly believes that if ever caught, he should be punished less if all he was doing was fucking some other bitches.

A *woman* don't have them same standards...for her the rules are completely different. For her it's almost the *opposite.* If she looked elsewhere for some mental stimulation...hell, even it was financially speaking...ain't no real violation in that. Yea, it's misogynistic, but I can forgive you if you cheated in a non-physical form. However, if she gave the nigga the pussy...now she's crossed a line that she can never turn around from. She done gave that other man exactly what he wanted...he wins, she loses. A cheating woman chooses the bigger of the two evils, if she chooses to give up the goods.

So it *does* matter if KeLLy fucked TJ...it's a key factor in this *whole* equation. But I can't let *her* know that.

"Rodney, look at me," she interrupts my thoughts. "You *know* me. Hell – you caught me up. I'm putting it all on the table, I'm trying to talk to you about this. I'll tell you what you wanna know...*whatever* you wanna know. Just don't leave like this. Don't just throw us away. Talk to me."

"*You* threw us away," I blamed her.

"*How,* baby?" she asked innocently. "I didn't have

sex with him."

"Tonight?"

"*Ever.*"

"Not *yet*," I assumed. "You *wanted* to. You would have. I *know* you was going to."

KeLLy paused, "Ok. But we hadn't done it."

"See," I felt my jaws tighten. "I'm done talking."

I start throwing more clothes in the trash bag…it's damn near full now. As I walk toward the kitchen, KeLLy is right behind me, "Rodney…talk to me. I'm telling you the truth now. We didn't have *sex*. What do you wanna know?"

"Man, you really expect me to believe y'all ain't fuck?" I cried out. "Then what the fuck you been doing with the nigga, Kells? Y'all been talking since *when*? I know before Thanksgiving, cuz that's why you tripped off me picking up yo phone. How long y'all been talking?"

"Since right after Halloween," she replied immediately.

I stopped and let it sink in…what she said.

"Didn't we get into a fight on Halloween?" I asked her as if I didn't remember.

KeLLy sighed before explaining, "Yes, Rodney. Because I wanted to go to the costume party that you didn't wanna dress up for, and then you ended up going to the party with yo bruhs instead of me!"

"Right. Ok, so we got into it and you went and found some side dick," I shook my head in disgust.

"We *didn't* have sex…"

"Whatever," I knew she was lying. "So you been talking to this nigga for a month and a half….and he ain't hit?"

"Don't say it like that," she was offended.

"Fuck that shit, Kells…answer the *gotdamn* question," I demanded. "You wanna talk….so talk."

"No he didn't '*hit*'," she answered my question reluctantly.

"Shit, *I* hit before the two-week mark," I reminded her. "And *I* was the side nigga when *we* started talking."

Kells turned her nose up, "Ugh…you an asshole!"

"Oh, we *name* calling now?!?!" I got louder. "Bitch, you got some nerve."

"*Wow*," she paused. "Ok. I deserve that."

"You damn right, bitch. You deserve that!"

"Now, Rodney," she urged. "Don't get carried away!"

"Man *fuck* you," I grunted back. "*Bitch.*"

She stands there in silence, in shock. I've never talked to her like this. She can feel the pain in my voice, she can see the tears in my eyes. She knows this one cut me deep. But KeLLy is still KeLLy. And she doesn't take well to the disrespect.

"Ok," she changed her tone. "See. That's what I'm talking about right there."

"What, KeLLy?" I exclaimed. "*What* the fuck are you talking about? You want me to believe you didn't fuck this nigga? That y'all was just cuddling and *talking* all this fucking time?!?! I don't understand how the fuck *you* got the nerve to be upset after all dis shit!"

"I don't see how you acting like you so innocent!" she threw at me.

"Don't turn this around on me, Kells! I ain't the one who just got caught at some other muhfuckaz house!"

"Ok you didn't get caught but I *know* you got other bitches, Rodney!" she yelled in frustration before lowering her voice again. "You can't help it...I know you do. I can't prove it, but I know you do."

"Get the fuck outta here...you sound stupid trying to turn the blame on me," I told her. "You don't even know what the fuck you talking about, bro!"

"I'm not *stupid,* nigga!!" she snapped at me. "Don't try to play me like I'm just dumb! Since we putting everything on the table, let's do *that.* I can *tell* you talk to other hoes! Whether I can prove it or *not*...I know you do!"

"Then, why are you with me then, Kells?" I asked rhetorically. "If you say I got other bitches, then why the fuck are you with me??? You sound stupid."

"Because I love you," she said matter-of-factly. "And I love the way you *used* to treat me."

"Oh, so now I don't *treat* you the same," I was triggered. "First I got other *bitches*...now I don't treat you the same. How many other excuses you got to get some other dick?!?!?"

Kells shook her head, "I don't know how many times I gotta say it, *we didn't have sex!*"

"I don't treat you the same, Kelly?" I went back to her claim, ignoring her lies about fucking TJ.

"You don't!" she reiterated. "You used to make me feel like nothing else mattered. You used to just be so sweet to me..."

"And now I'm not?" I couldn't believe what she was saying. "I feel like a sweet, ole, sucka-for-love ass nigga right *now.* I tell you dat much."

"That's cuz you hurt right now. But it's not the same with us, Rodney, it ain't been the same all semester. You used to leave me little love notes all over the place...*all the time*. That used to just *make my day*! The *poems* you used to write me.

"How you would surprise me with dinner...surprise deliveries. Every other *day*...every other *week*! You used to make me feel so *special,* Rodney."

I couldn't stop shaking my head in disagreement, "Man, you acting like I don't do *none* of that shit no more! Damn, you know I been taking classes again! The fuck?!"

"*So what?* That never stopped you before!" Kells shot back. "When's the last time you gave me a *massage?* Or a *foot rub?*"

This took my frustration through the roof. I started ranting passionately, "See you on some fucking bullshit...I never even rubbed a chick's feet before *you* for real!!! Like are you even *serious* right now?!?! You coming up with all these excuses for why you been creeping around?!?! *Really?*"

"I'm just telling you," she responded calmly. "You *know* how I feel about you, Rodney! How I break my fucking neck and back to make sure *you* happy and taken care of! You been kicking it ever since we got back to the Burg and *hell* – you give yo *bruhs* more attention than you do me!"

"So, now you wanna compete with my bruhs again,"

I sighed. Not this again.

"No, that's *not* what I'm saying," she stopped me. "I'm saying you know I like to feel special. *Appreciated.* And you know better than *anybody* how to make me feel like that...you know *ME*, Rodney. So why don't you? Why let me feel unappreciated lately? You ever stop to think about *why* I would be doing all this?"

"I know why," I replied sharply. "Cuz you want some other dick."

"See, there you go being an ass again," Kells was disappointed I took it back there.

"So y'all ain't fuck?"

"No."

"Did y'all kiss?"

She hesitated.

"You said whatever I wanna know," I smirked.

"Ok," her shoulders sunk in. "Yes."

"Oh wow!" my eyes widened. "And I complain that you don't kiss me enough?!?!? *Wow.* Unbelievable. I thought you ain't *like* to kiss, Kells..."

"No, I said that I just have to get *used* to the way you kiss me so much," she tried to explain. "My last boyfriend

78

wasn't a kisser. It's the way *you* kiss…"

"So now I can't kiss?" I had to smile to keep my cool. My blood was boiling and that stinging feeling in my heart had returned.

"I didn't say that," Kells said softly, obviously trying to lessen the blows.

"Y'all seen each other naked? Y'all touched?"

She looked at me with puppy eyes, "Rodney…"

"Have you grabbed his dick or has he touched yo pussy?" I kept going.

KeLLy sighed again, "*Yes*. But we didn't have sex."

"You suck his dick?"

"I'm not gonna answer that," she looked away, now more offended than before.

I didn't care. I knew I had pushed her buttons, and I wasn't backing down. I started clapping my hands as I yelled from the depths of my soul, "WHAT THE FUCK YOU MEAN?!?!? DID – YOU – SUCK – HIS – DICK?!?!?!

* * * * *

10

KeLLy stood there in silence, looking off into space. I dropped the trash bag and fold my arms. She ain't getting outta this one. I have to know. I know what I heard...which I ain't even told her about yet. But when it comes to *my* principles on **cheating** – I ain't really got her caught red-handed. She gotta confess some shit...or prove some shit wrong if it ain't true.

And in all honesty – it's really about *me* proving the rumors *right* – the burden of proof lies with the *accuser*. And I know all of this. *KeLLy* knows all of this because we used to **cheat** together. This stand-off is getting crazy.

She knows I don't really wanna leave. But she also knows that I will. My pride is hurt. If she's developed a desire to *cheat* because she's unhappy or feeling under-appreciated...then it may be too late anyway. Once a woman is done and is ready to move on...she's OUTTA DER□. I haven't been able to determine if that's the case with KeLLy...but I don't want to stick around if it is. My pride won't let me.

"So you not gon answer?!?!" I asked after the most awkward of silences.

"I don't like you talking to me like that," she replied tight-lipped.

"You not in a position to '*like*' how you being talked to! *HELLO*?!?!?! I just caught you over the nigga's crib at 1 in the fuckin *morning*! You talmbout you ain't *fuck* him – I just wanna know what *did* you do then? Did you *suck* him up or not???"

She takes a seat on the tan-colored living room couch. She's really not trying to answer the shit.

"You know what, fuck it – it's cool," I gave up. It didn't matter anyway. "I know you fucked that nigga anyway. I'm sure you sucked him off."

"Fuck you, Rodney."

"Fuck *me???*" I give her the head nod and walk to the corner of the room to start unhooking my *Dell* computer. I just need to get all the rest of my shit and go. I'm done talking.

"How you '*think*' you know?" she tried to spark the conversation back up just that quickly.

"It don't even matter – I know" I refused to play her mind game. "I caught yo ass, didn't I?!?!"

"I mean," she paused briefly. "Whatever nigga. I don't see how you think you know I fucked him. Cuz I *didn't*. And you can't prove I *did*."

I keep unscrewing the monitor from the tower…marinating on what she just said. I can't stand her ass right now. But at the same time…this shit fucks with me. She sounds like *me*. I'm getting a taste of my own remedy for the first time ever….and though it's not as belligerent as I tend to get, it's giving me a rush.☐

"Oh yeah, you don't have nothing to say now, huh?" she knew she had pushed another button. "Ain't that what you always be saying? Prove it?"

"KeLLy, stop talking to me. You full of shit!" I shouted.

She knows she's under *my* skin now. This time, it's her turn to keep pressing, "Oh, I'm full of shit?! Was I full of shit when I was taking yo ass to work every damn day last year? Was I full of shit when I took *care* of yo ass – made sure you was fed *and* had clean clothes?! I'm full of shit *now* cuz I got some attention *elsewhere*? You ain't been giving me none!"

My breathing speeds up…and I can't move fast enough. I gotta get outta here before I say something I regret. Or do something crazy…after I told my ship I wouldn't.

But she's really pushing my buttons now, ranting, "You know what I'm saying – what about *me?!?!* I cater to you night and day around here! When is the last time we went on a *date,* Rodney??? I shouldn't have to rely on some other man to do yo job!!!"

This bitch. Keep moving Rod.

"And now you just wanna leave?!?! How weak is that?!?! You just gonna give up now? After all this???"

I pick my computer up and start walking to the front door. I just need to start packing my car. It's getting harder and harder to hold back the tears.

"Rodney, if you leave…don't come back. You walk out on us…it's over," she threatened.

"That's what you want anyway," I mumbled. "It was over when you lied to get me out the house and outta town…"

"I didn't *lie* to get you outta town. You wanted to see yo family."

"Then why am I back in the *Burg,* KeLLy, if that was the case?"

I don't wait for a response, I'm already outside and loading my car now. KeLLy is standing in the doorway, still going off. She's done a great job of turning this shit around on me. And maybe it serves me right. But still…it hurts. It hurts like fuckin' hell. It feels like there's a hole in the middle of my heart…it's almost hard to breathe. All that shit she talked about not making her look like a fool….and then she turns around and starts fucking with a nigga around the corner. I mean, she been seen with this nigga on campus – I got muhfuckaz *asking* me about this nigga! This shit hurts so *bad*...I feel like I've been tricked.

As I walk back in to get some more of my things, KeLLy stands in the doorway...purposely bumping into me as I stroll past her. I just shake my head. She really trying me.

"KeLLy, gone somewhere! You keep trying to test me."

"So you leaving me, Rodney???" she sounded fake-shocked.

"Why would I stay?!?!" I couldn't hide my emotion. "All that shit you talk – and yet you got me out here looking like a fool! I hate you."

"No, you don't" she reasoned with me. "I know you love me, Rodney. That's why you so hurt."

My bottom lip shook, "Man, you got me looking like a fool out here."

"No, I don't!" she disagreed with irritation. "I didn't have sex...and it ain't like people running around here talking about it."

"That's what you think!" I hmphed.

"*Who?* Who's talking about it?" she challenged.

"I mean, you ain't even wondered how the fuck I

knew what was up? How I found yo ass?!?!" I shook my head at her arrogance. "Damn Kells...you real cocky right now."

"What are you saying?" she wanted to know. "I mean, I don't get it...spit it out! Cuz I know don't nobody know what's been going on and *he* damn sure ain't said shit."

"Would you bet that?" I eyeballed her. "I wouldn't."

"Well, what do you think you know? I know he ain't said nothing..."

"He *did,* dumbass!!!! He out here talking about how he hit it from the back...bragging n'shit!!!!"

"That's a lie...and I know *TJ* ain't said that shit. So who told you that???"

"Don't even trip," I told her. "He said the shit. That's why I got on the fuckin highway and caught yo ass! You got *sloppy*...and yo boy running his mouth."

"Well ,that's a lie," she didn't believe me. "I don't know why he would say that. And I can't see him saying that cuz we never had sex."

"So, you taking up for him now?" I was taken aback. "*Wow*. Ok. Lemme get the rest of my shit! You off the chain, KeLLy."

"I wanna know who told you that."

I ignore her and try to get the rest of my shit without talking anymore. There's so much I wanna say to her. But right now, I just can't. It's almost 3 in the morning…and I need to try to figure out what I'm gonna do with my life now. I can't stay in this house anymore…I don't even wanna stay in *the Burg* anymore. I start thinking about how many steps backwards I'd be taking if I leave. I really have nowhere to go.

I'm enrolled in the *Criminal Justice* grad program and working part time at *Office Depot*…all of my livelihood is here in Warrensburg now. I mean, if I go back to the city, I'll be living at my aunt's house unemployed. KeLLy was truly my lifeline right now. If I throw this shit away…I have no idea which way I'll be able to move. Ain't no real plan. This is all full of impulsive emotion. And right now, I'm overcome with it.

The tears start flowing everywhere now as I'm walking back and forth to my car…loading it up. It's to the point now where I'm not even throwing shit in bags…just grabbing and tossing in the back seat or trunk – wherever shit will fit.

KeLLy continues to try to push my buttons…but now that I'm crying…it's easier to ignore her. As I finish cramming my car, she tries to stop me one last time. But I yank away from her and tell her I never wanna see her again. I see a tear forming in her eye as I say it…and I turn around and hurry out before it drops.

One thing I can't handle is seeing KeLLy cry. But I must stand my ground in this moment, at all costs.

"Goodbye, KeLLy."

*   *   *   *   *

By the time I pull in J Dub's parking lot again...I'm balling like a little girl. I'm talking snot-running, sniffling, and crazy breathing...the shit is starting to really sink in.

I think about calling her...but I don't know what I would say. I'm torn...conflicted with my emotion versus my pride. I can't let her know she's got the best of me. I wanna forget about all of this and act like it never happened. But how is that even possible? It's just not. I'ma forever be haunted by images of her getting the dick – I can hear her *moaning* and *splashing* everywhere. It's making my stomach cringe.

Before I can take another breath...I've got the driver door open and throwing up...vomiting all over the ground next to my car. I ain't never felt this type of sickness. I'm in desperate need of help...yet I don't know what kind of help, or where to get it.

When something close to this happened to any of my other friends...they called their parents – somebody close who knew 'em. My mom is out...she's been dead since I was 14. I know my Pops is the best person to talk to overall. Pops always gives me good advice and most of the time can tell me a story that directly relates to whatever I'm going through. But shit, I know he sleep by now. The ringer prolly off at this hour so I'ma have to wait til I geet to the city tomorrow to have our long talk.

88

But I need to talk to somebody *now*.

I'm losing my mind...

Without another thought...I pull my phone out. The battery is near dead, but there's enough juice for me to get one last phone call in. I dial the number out...I know this one by heart. After three rings, they pick up on the other end.

"Hello???" I sniffled. "*Miss Fischer??* I'm sorry to wake you up, but I really need to talk to somebody right now..."

*   *   *   *   *

11

"*Rodney?*" Miss Fischer recognizes my voice, though she sounds startled to hear from me

"Yes…it's me," I replied through my tears.

"What's wrong, Rodney? It's 3 something in the morning."

"I know, I'm sorry…I'm sorry. I didn't know who else to call."

Miss Fischer sighed, "Ok, Mr. Henderson…I'm sitting up now. What happened?"

I didn't get along with KeLLy's mom *at all*. We constantly stayed at each other's throats and I was unlike anybody her daughter had ever been involved with. Every time I saw or talked to her there was a debate or disagreement about *something*. She was my biggest hater in this situation…and I ain't expect her to really talk to me.

But she did.

I poured my heart out to Mrs. Fischer that night. Told her how I hadn't been perfect, but also how much I loved her daughter and how hurt I was to catch her with somebody else. I told her about everything...how KeLLy wouldn't come outside at first, how she started throwing shit up in my face when I questioned her. She was so empathetic...I had never known that side of her. I mean, she got out of bed with her husband to talk to me after 3 in the morning.

She told me how it was no secret that she wasn't a fan of Kells and I...but she respected me for being who I was to her, and she knew I loved her daughter. Miss Fischer felt like maybe we were moving too fast to be so young...and maybe KeLLy needs to realize what she really wants. She suggested that I give her some serious space and if we end up back together...then so be it.

"Well, she says they never had sex," I explained. "I don't believe her though."

"Well hey, I know my daughter is sexually active. Both my daughters are and I'm not proud of it and they know I do not approve," she made herself clear. "But I did raise them to be respectful. So, I don't know Rodney, if that's what she says...maybe she's telling the truth. Or maybe she's lying to protect your feelings.

"You have to ask yourself is that all that matters, and will you be done with her *if so*. If that's the case...then walk away and never look back. But I know you love her. Any fool that will call somebody's mama at almost 4 in the morning is wide open...I mean, come on now, Mr. Henderson."

"You right – I do," I sniffed again, wiping my tears from my chin. "I love KeLLy, Miss Fischer."

"Well, she loves you too," she reassured me with empathy. "I know she does. And I know you don't believe it, but *I* love you too Rodney. I don't hate you like you say I do. I look at you like a son, the same way I look at my own. You get on my nerves just the same."

Though I was sure I already looked a mess from all the crying, I was happy she couldn't see me blushing. Trying not to sound embarrassed, I finally told her, "Thank you Miss Fischer. I really appreciate this. Thank you…"

"You're welcome, anytime you need to talk. Just try not to do it in the middle of the night like this again, ok? And get you some rest. I know you've been drinking – I smell it through the phone."

I forced a smile…and thanked KeLLy's mom again. I'm not sure what all that call accomplished…but it did make me feel a little better.

Maybe space was what we both needed.

J Dub left the door unlocked for me, and I crashed on his couch…but I didn't get much sleep at all. Too many nightmares, haunting images. As soon as 8:30 hit, I was on the highway…on my way back to Kansas City. For good.

*   *   *   *   *

So later that Sunday…I'm visiting my *Pops*, watching

93

the *Chiefs* play the *Broncos*. I tell him what happened, and
he tells me he thinks I'll take her back. He likes
KeLLy…he thinks she's good for me.

"Ok well, tell me this, son," he said. "Whoever told
you they heard this guy in the weight room…how you
know they telling the truth??"

"I mean, I just do, Pops," I couldn't explain it, but I
just knew. "It's too much of a coincidence. And why
would a nigga lie about smashing? That don't even add
up."

Pops looked up at the ceiling, rubbing his chin,
"I'ma tell you like this, Lil Rod – some of these guys out
here will lie on they dick like that…trying to be with the
cool cats. Maybe…now I'm just saying *maybe*…she didn't
give it up yet."

"Yeah, but she *wanted* to, Pop!!! She even said it
herself…she was gonna give him some. I know it, dude. If
I didn't catch her ass…I mean, my bad. If I ain't catch her
butt in the act…he'a probably still be up in it right now!!!"

Pops started screaming at the tv, "*Are you kidding
me?!?!* So nobody is tackling this guy today?!?!?!"

Clinton Portis was lighting the *Chiefs* and just tied his
record of 4 rushing touchdowns in a game vs KC. He
could break the record if he got another 1 before the game
was over. I hopped up and started cheering loudly – hand
in my dad's face, "Yea, let's go! That's what I'm talking
about!!!! *Mile High Salute*, nigga!!!"

94

Watching football with Pops was something I hadn't been able to do in a minute…and that also helped me feel better. Suddenly I didn't feel so down. Being around people who you know care about you is sometimes the perfect cure for a broken heart.

"So are you gonna call her?" Pops wondered.

"What for?" I didn't see a point.

"I'm telling you – this is just another lesson for you to learn about the *Curse*. You not getting rid of her that easily, so you just need to put your brain at ease." He advised me. "Ok, now this what you do, son. Call her up, out the blue. Wait 'til tomorrow since you said you not going to work. Wait, now hold on, are you just gonna *quit yo job* now son?"

I thought about it for a second, "Man…I don't know. I can't go back down there."

He gave me a stern look, "Ok…you better figure *that* out boy. But look – you call her tomorrow and you tell her to call that nigga on the 3-way. You stay quiet. Tell her to start talking to that nigga about how good it was…and pay attention to how he react. If she's telling the truth about that…you'll know then. But you gotta make her call him right then and there, Junior."

Hmm. Good idea Pops.

As long as she ain't already anticipated this and they both got a chance to be on one accord. I'm still wrestling with why them fucking or not matters so damn much. I know it was her intent…but if it never actually happened yet…then it's just easier for me to swallow. No matter how many times I ask myself this, I end up at that same conclusion. With the way I'm out here doing my thing…I gotta be able to forgive her if she ain't gave it up yet. Right??

*   *   *   *   *

Monday Night

KeLLy had been calling me non-stop since I left, and I've refused to talk. All day long, I've kept the same CD in my car stereo. Same song on repeat….re-pumping all the testosterone back into my blood. I've been sitting in my car in my aunt's driveway for hours. Heat on blast with the window cracked. Smoking my life away, drinking gin and pineapple juice. Once I got good and full…I headed back into the house, on my mission.

The living room was empty, as usual. So it was now or never. I pulled out my phone and settled in on the sectional couch.

"Hello?" she answered after the first ring.

"Are you busy?" I asked, clearing my throat.

"No, Rodney. I've been calling you."

Hearing her voice suddenly makes me hear my heart

beating again. I closed my eyes and took a deep breath, "Well, I called you back. So let's talk."

"I want you *home*," she told me bluntly before I could say another word.

"I'm not coming home, Kelly."

"Baby, listen…we can work this out," she spoke with conviction. "We can work on us. Come home."

"I don't want to come home!" I cried out. "We can try…to work this out. But that's not gonna happen overnight. Like…you have to realize how this shit is affecting me."

"I know…I know," she sounded sad. "Because I know how I would feel if the tables were turned. I'm sorry. I really am sorry that this had to happen. I'm sorry I did this to you."

She can't see 'em coming down my eyes…and I take a deep sigh.

Kells continues, "Rodney, I do love you. I'm not perfect. You know that. You knew that about me and that's why I love you. That's why we love each other. We both take the good with the bad. I'm really sorry…"

All I could think about suddenly was her in TJ's bed. My throat felt dry, as I managed to utter, "Man you gave this nigga my *pussy,* man."

97

"No, I *didn't*…quit saying it like that!" she snapped at me defensively. "Rodney, I'm telling you the *truth*…I did not have sex with that boy. I would have. I was *going* to…*ok*? But I didn't! You stopped that."

"*Whatever.*"

"You did. You drove on the highway, in the middle of the night and damn near kicked the door in!" she chuckled. "I'm sorry…I know it's not funny. But if you coulda saw the look on my face…I said *oh shit! The rent is due!!!!*"

We both can't help but laugh for a moment, but I quickly catch myself, "What all did you do with him? Period."

"I did *not* suck his dick. I cannot believe you asked me that. You know how long it took me to give you head??? I mean – come on now."

"You played wit it?" I asked blatantly with no hesitation.

"I did."

"You wanted to fuck that nigga," I bit my lip.

"Yes, I told you," she admitted. "But I knew that if it happened…it would change us forever. I hadn't brought myself to doing it, and it obviously wasn't meant to go down."

"You talked to him since? How I know you ain't with him right now?" I asked her as my heartbeat sped up. "Yesterday you couldn't wait for me to leave town so you could spend the night with that nigga, man."

"He is not over here, Rodney," she shot back. "That was the first time I was gonna spend the night with him. Hell, I'm with you *all the time*...when could I have spent the night with him???"

I wasn't falling for the logic, "Man, y'all coulda been doing quickies n'shit...I ain't with you *every* moment. I know you Kells, you know how long we was creeping before you broke up with *Jamal*???"

"Ok, but I'm *telling* you!" she cried. "I did *not*...have *sex* with him."

"Have you talked to him?"

"He doesn't want to talk to me after all'at."

"Have you *talked* to him?" I repeated myself with emphasis. "You tried to call him?"

"I did, and we talked for maybe 2 minutes after you left last night," Kells confessed. "He said he didn't wanna have anything to do with me anymore."

"Call him," I instructed her.

"No, I'm not calling him!" she responded quickly, raising her voice. "*For what*? I'm talking to my man."

"No, you not," I rolled my eyes. "Call him, and I'ma be quiet. I want you to call him on the other line…and start talking to him about y'all having sex."

"*What,* boy???"

"Click over…call that nigga," I said slowly, letting her know I was serious. "And I wanna listen to y'all talk. I want *you* – to start off talking about how y'all had sex. I wanna see what *he* says. How he responds."

She smacked her lips, "But, we didn't *have* sex, Rodn…"

"Ok, well then he gon be confused," I cut her off. "I'll know the truth then. Call him."

Kells thought about it for a second, "If I do this, are you gon come home and we be done with this?"

"No," I killed that idea. "But I'll know you're not lying about *that*. After that…we'll see. But I'm not coming home…we need to work on us. This is a start."

"Ok, Rodney."

"Ok what?" I asked her to clarify.

"Hold on…lemme call him," she replied calmly.

"Aye!" I got loud. "You better click *right* back over, too."

"Boy I'm *not* 'bout to try to clue him in," Kells knew what I was thinking. "I'm not lying to you. I'ma do what you asking. If this gon make you feel better…so be it. Now *HOLD. ON.*"

*   *   *   *   *

12

She had me on hold for only 15 seconds or so. But it felt like it was the longest 15 seconds of my young life. When she finally clicked back over, her and him were already conversing.

"…was sorry. I understand if you don't wanna keep going, that's cool," she said. "But are we good? I don't want you having any type of beef with me about it."

"Nah…it's good," TJ whispered. He sounded half-sleep. "Shit fucked up…but's all good."

"So why you tell yo boy how my shit *feel?* That's what I'm tryna get."

TJ yawned, "Maaan, I don't know why he say that."

"I mean, I know niggaz talk," Kells said, trying to get him to open up. "But why say *that?* If you really don't know how I feel yet?"

"I'm saying it *woulda* been cool…if it went down like that, that's all I was saying," he explained.

"Well, why did you even say that then…if you knew we ain't did it?" she asked him.

"Aye, it's all good," he ignored the question. I had to strain to hear him, his voice sounded muffled. Then he started speaking indistinctively, "I mean...*ole dude*...I ain't wit that shit, bruh. You do you. No problem wit you – you good. Be with yo man, that's all I'm saying."

KeLLy sighed, as if she could also barely make out what he was saying, "Ok, well I'll let you go back to sleep, TJ. I just wanted to ask that."

"Aight, holla," he hung up.

*   *   *   *   *

KeLLy tries to click back over but hangs me up in the process. I take another sip from my juice bottle before she calls back.

"Yeah."

"Ok," she clears her throat. "Were you listening?"

"I heard him."

"So do you believe me now?"

"I don't know," I sighed. I still had so many questions and didn't know where to begin. I stuttered, "I..I don't know. Shit, it sound like you done already talked to him about what I said he said."

KeLLy got defensive, "Ok *yes* – you damn right I asked him about that shit cuz I don't understand why he would say that shit! That nigga *know* we ain't did it yet. Ok?

"So when I talked to him after you bounced, I asked him why the fuck he would say the shit and he ain't have no answer this morning just like he ain't have no answer just now. So now – *do* you believe me?"

"Man, you ain't gotta raise yo voice at me," I attempted to regain the upper hand. "I don't know. Why wouldn't you tell me you had already asked him about it?"

She started rambling and running her sentences together, "Cuz you just told me to call him and you was so *set* on how you wanted me to talk to him…and we don't even talk like that Rodney. *Ok?* So I didn't tell you I already asked him why he lied. *So what?* I'm telling the truth about fucking him. I didn't fuck dat nigga."

"But why keep that from me though?"

"Rodney, you act like you telling me *everything* about all this!" she got defensive again. "You won't even tell me *who* told you he said that bullshit!! Who told you that, Rodney?"

"Don't worry about it," I refused to play it her way, "It don't matter."

"Ok, well *that* don't matter either, then," she met me with sarcasm. "Are you coming home now?"

"No," I told her. "But maybe I believe you."

"Rodney. I miss you."

"Whatever."

"You don't miss me?"

"I do," I had to admit.

"Then come *home*," she urged.

"Nah. We need space right now."

"Just come down here. You ain't gotta stay or move back in. I need to see you," she persisted.

"For what?" I spat back.

KeLLy lowered her voice, making her hint more obvious, "Rodney..."

Shit.

She had me right where she wanted me and I knew it. Without hesitation, I replied, "Ok, I'm on my way. But I'm not staying."

"Ok, long as you not leaving either," she sounded like she was smiling.

"Don't push it, Kells. I'm not staying *for real.*"

"You not gon spend the night with me?"

"*Tonight?*" I pondered aloud. "Yeah."

"Ok, that's all I need right now. I'll take it," she confirmed excitedly. "Be careful…call me when you're close."

*   *   *   *   *

It's hard to walk away from any relationship….and Kells had my heart. So I couldn't leave her alone completely, but I did plan on giving us space.

That was the last time I lived in the Burg. After that, I dropped out of grad school and stayed in KC to jumpstart my corporate career. KeLLy stayed close, though…putting in serious work to win me back. And I'm talking serious work. If she ever treated me good before, after this shit – she started treating me like a KING. She refused to let us go…she said she knew where she belonged.

After a while, it started to weigh on me. I mean I felt bad. I felt bad because whether she fucked TJ or not – at the end of the day, she couldn't possibly have been on the level of cheating that I had been on in this relationship. In life *period*. Who am I to cast her away for committing half of my sins? That shit stayed on my mind and on my heart the entire *four months* KeLLy was on my heels after that…before I ended up agreeing to give it a serious second shot.

*   *   *   *   *

April 2004

At the end of that next spring semester...I asked KeLLy to move back to KC...with me. She laid next to me in bed, in tears and disbelief. She asked me why...she really wanted to know.

And so I decided to tell her.

I ain't tell her about all the *cheating* I was doing and how that was killing my conscience. Nah...she ain't need to know all'at. She only needed to get the message. She only needed to know of a portion of my cheating...so she could understand my guilt.

The Art of Cheating is an art indeed – let's be clear about that much. Sometimes, you gotta give up a little...to get away with a lot. Some things you gotta take on the chin...for the greater cause. *KeLLy's Revenge* was full of the purest energy behind *The Art*.

She wanted to know *why* I eventually took her back...and so one late night, I gathered up the nerve to tell her the necessary half-truth.

"I'm tryna confess something, Kelly."

"Ok, you told me to brace myself...and we're gonna be honest moving forward," Kells gathered herself. "Ok. I'm ready."

I took a long, deep breath. What I had to tell Kells was tough and I didn't know exactly where to begin. So, I counted to three in my head, and just came out with it, "Ok, so that night after we called him on the three-way and I got in the shower before I came down to see you…"

"Go on," she folded her arms. "I'm listening."

"I told you I had to take my cousin to the store first," I took her back to that night we made up. "Well really…I was on the phone with the person who told me what TJ said in the gym."

KeLLy cut her eyes at me in the darkness, "I see. Ok…so *who* was it?"

*   *   *   *   *

December 2003

I was still in my towel, fresh out the shower. I needed to leave soon, and so I had to call her back. She just wouldn't stop calling me about this shit. She was yelling on the other end of the phone…mad as fuck. Cursing even, and she *never* cursed. She was seriously in her feelings about the fact that I was on my way to see *KeLLy*…even though I explained to her that I wuttin' necessarily 'bout to take her back.

I had told her how I believed KeLLy ain't fuck TJ. She thought I was a fool for that. I told her how I had them on the three-way and how I heard him halfway admit to just talking shit…and she got even *more* upset. She couldn't believe that after everything I had taught *her*

109

about *The Art of Cheating*...how I could fall for such tricks. She wanted to know how KeLLy had my heart like that...she knew I wuttin' pussy-whipped off KeLLy cuz I couldn't get enough of fucking the shit outta *her*. She wanted me to say, *'fuck going to see KeLLy'* and instead come see *her* when I got to the Burg that night. She couldn't understand how I could go back to KeLLy when she was kissing TJ...knowing how much I loved to kiss. Knowing how much she kissed me the way KeLLy wouldn't. She wanted answers...

So, there I stood, towel wrapped around my body, having a heated argument with my side chick – my mistress in every sense of the word...*Cookie*.

Cookie wanted answers...and she demanded them now.

"Look, I don't know what else you want me to say," I told her as I lotioned my chest. "You know how I feel about her."

"Ok, and?!" Cookie screamed in the phone. "You know how I feel about *Skates* and every time you ask me to sneak away from him...do I hesitate?"

"Cookie...come on," I hung my head, trying to remain calm. "Be cool..."

"You full of shit, Rodney!" she cursed at me. Cookie never cursed, let alone at me. She was pissed, "You let her run all over you for real...and you know it! You know she fucked that nigga! You know she lying, they prolly still

110

fucking! I heard that nigga telling Skates that shit…I was standing right there!"

"Ok," I paused. "So maybe she did…maybe she didn't! How can I be mad at her with this shit I got going on with you???"

"Whatever! Me and you was fucking way before KeLLy came into the picture! And she had a boyfriend anyway! Oh my God, you are so stupid when it come to her! I cannot believe you!"

I shook my head, "Cookie look…you starting to sound real jealous. Don't do this. Why are you so mad about it now? Like you said…you been around since *before* KeLLy. Why are you acting like this now??"

"Cuz I hate to see her do you like this, *Rodney*! I do. And you know how I feel about you…but you just always put her on a pedestal over me," she sighed. Then her voice softened and lowered, "Just come see me, for real baby."

"No, Cookie. I need to sort all this shit out. Just stay cool and lemme figure some shit out."

"You're gon get back with her," the disappointment in her tone was loud and clear.

"No, I'm not," I tried to convince her. "Not yet. Look…chill…you gotta chill, dude. I'ma talk to you later. I gotta go."

*   *   *   *   *

Like I said before, *The Art of Cheating* is real. You never think it could happen to you, but *KeLLy's Revenge* was served on a cold platter, like any revenge should always be served. Ahhhhh...but no one ever stops to ask...who is the *waitress* that's serving???

Props to Cookie, ***my main side chick***. And props to all the other amazingly loyal side chicks holding it down out there. You know who you are. If it wuttin' for y'all, we all might be clueless in this crazy world filled with lies, lust, and madness.

Especially...when the tables turn.

FIN.
(Until We Cheat Again)

ABOUT THE AUTHOR

"*HoLLyRod*" – the author & creator of the highly controversial and raunchy storyline, *The Art of Cheating* – is the alter-ego and pseudonym for established writer Rodney L. Henderson Jr.

Since graduating with a Business Administration degree in Computer Information Systems from the *University of Central Missouri*, Henderson has showcased his writing skills in various forms of art – including radio commercials & music, as well as poetry & promo spots for fashion companies such as *DymeWear Inc & Ridikulus Kouture LLC.*

HoLLyRod's short story mini-series titled ***The Art of Cheating Episodes*** introduces readers to the many characters & mystery behind **HoLLyWorld** and *The Art of Cheating*, while chronicling the ups & downs of infidelity through experiences based on real life. The ongoing series has been re-released in a special Extended Author's Cut Edition.

AVAILABLE IN eBOOK & PAPERBACK FORMATS!!!
AUDIO BOOKS COMING SOON!!!

Henderson currently resides in his home state of Missouri and spends most of his time managing & writing for *Angela Marie Publishing, LLC* – a company named after his late mother.

The Art of Cheating Episodes is published under *Lurodica Stories*, an erotica division of the publishing company.

"*I just want to continue to be inspired at the notion of making her proud and keep my promise to share my talents with the world.*"

www.HoLLyRods.com
www.facebook.com/TheArtOfCheating
www.twitter.com/TheCheatGods

Next up on
The Art of Cheating...

SEASON 1 — EPISODE 5:
The HooKup

HoLLyRod has decided to take a break from KeLLy following her revenge episode. Determined to sort things out on his own, he's also cut off contact with his main side chick, Cookie. After moving back home to start over from scratch, HoLLy quickly realizes that getting hooKed up on blind dates rarely ever goes smoothly. But this new girl, Tianna, is supposed to be the perfect type of f*ck buddy to help take HoLLy's mind off things for a while. Still, in this new era of internet pages & profile pics, HoLLyRod knows he's taking a big shot in the dark at meeting up with this freak.
But this is The Art of Cheating, so then again - so is she...

EXTENDED AUTHOR'S CUT EDITION
AVAILABLE NOW

Also by HoLLyRod

The Art of Cheating Episodes
(Extended Author's Cut Edition)

SEASON 1
Episode 1 - Sassy
Episode 2 – Hangover
Episode 3 - HoLLy BeLLigerence
Episode 4 - KeLLy's Revenge
Episode 5 - The HooKup
Episode 6 – Ménages

SEASON 2
Episode 1 - Cyber Pimpin' **(12/22/22)**
Episode 2 - Campus Record **(2/15/23)**
Episode 3 – A Date with Karma **(4/20/23)**
Episode 4 – The Wedding Party **(6/19/23)**
Episode 5 – HoLLy & Sug **(8/23/23)**

SEASON 3
(Spring 2024)

Angela Marie Publishing
Presents

WDFFIL EP1: Facing the Music

The OFFICIAL Soundtrack to The Art of Cheating Episodes

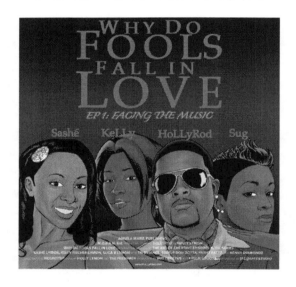

AVAILABLE ON ALL MUSIC PLATFORMS

DOWNLOAD OR STREAM NOW!!!!

https://distrokid.com/hyperfollow/hollyrod/wdffil-ep1-facing-the-music-4

Angela Marie Publishing, LLC. All rights reserved.

Made in the USA
Columbia, SC
16 July 2022